Ink

given to me by Barbie Boo
Feb. 1993 for my birthday

Ink and Strawberries

An Anthology of Quebec Women's Fiction

edited by
Beverley Daurio & Luise von Flotow

translated by
Luise von Flotow

Aya Press · Toronto

English translations copyright © Luise von Flotow and the authors, 1988
'Strawberry Time' copyright © Susanna Finnell and Suzanne Jacob, 1988

ALL RIGHTS RESERVED.

No part of this book may be reproduced in any form without the written permission of the publisher, with the exception of short passages for review purposes.

Published with the assistance of
the Canada Council and the Ontario Arts Council.

The translation of this book was made possible
by a grant from the Canada Council.

Cover: J. Paul McGarry
Production Co-ordination: The Blue Pencil
Typeset and printed at
The Coach House Press, Toronto

Aya Press
Box 1153, Station F
Toronto, Ontario
Canada M4Y 2T8

Canadian Cataloguing in Publication
Main entry under title:

Ink and strawberries : an anthology of Quebec women's fiction

ISBN 0-920544-57-6

1. Canadian fiction (French) – Women authors.*
2. Canadian fiction (French) – Quebec (Province).*
3. Canadian fiction (French) – Translations into English.*
4. English fiction – Translations from French.
I. Daurio, Beverley, 1953-   .
II. Von Flotow-Evans, Luise.

PS8329.5.Q4I63 1988   C843'.54'08092872   C88-093697-5
PQ3916.5.E6I63 1988

Acknowledgements

Thanks to Luise von Flotow, who initiated the project and has worked assiduously and with dedication towards its completion; to Robert Paquin; to Gwen Hoover; to Susanna Finnell; to Stéphane Hébert; to Loren MccRory; and especially to the writers.

'Tenderness,' Marie-Claire Blais: 'Tendresse', *La Vie en Rose*, July / August 1985

'Walking,' France Théoret: 'La Marche', *Nécessairement Putain*, Les Herbes Rouges, 1983

'Excerpt from *Picture Theory*,' Nicole Brossard: from *Picture Theory*, Montreal, 1982

'Henna for Luck,' Madeleine Ouellette-Michalska: 'Du henné pour la chance,' *La Femme de Sable*, Editions Naaman, 1978

'Strawberry Time,' Suzanne Jacob: 'Le temps des fraises,' Biocreux Inc., 1979

'128 Park Avenue,' Hélène Le Beau: '128 Park Avenoo,' *La Vie en Rose*, Vol. 4, 1985

'Subversion and Passion,' Danielle Drouin: 'Subversion et passion,' *Moebius*, No. 22, 1984

'Journey,' Louise Coiteux: *Moebius*, No. 22, 1984

'The Story of,' Lori Saint-Martin: 'Histoire de', *Nouvelle Barre du Jour*, April, 1986

'Sunday,' Carol Dunlop: 'Dimanche,' *Liberté*, Vol. 21, No. 122, 1979

'As Moist as Montreal,' Anne Dandurand: 'Montréal Moite,' *XYZ*, No. 8, Winter 1986

The above stories used by permission of the authors or their executors. *Every effort has been made to ascertain copyright ownership and to obtain permission for material in this book.*

Contents

Strawberry Time *Suzanne Jacob.*
Translated by Susanna Finnell. 9

Stories *Colette Tougas* 19

128 Park Avenue *Hélène Le Beau* 27

Henna for Luck *Madeleine Ouellette-Michalska* 31

Tenderness *Marie-Claire Blais* 39

The Story of *Lori Saint-Martin* 42

It Would Be Night *Claire Dé* 45

Ink-Stained Love *Anne Dandurand* 52

As Moist as Montreal *Anne Dandurand* 53

Journey *Louise Coiteux* 55

Subversion and Passion: Reflections, Wanderings
Danielle Drouin 58

Walking *France Théoret* 68

Sunday *Carol Dunlop* 71

Excerpt from **Picture Theory** *Nicole Brossard* 75

Notes on the Contributors 91

Strawberry Time

Suzanne Jacob

I was holding them in my hands so I had to open the door in a complicated way with my elbows and knees, finally kicking it shut. I ran to the kitchen. Our kitchen has a swing door without handles. I sent it slamming into the green chimney. My mother always says that I am too noisy, my movements too sweeping, my mouth too big, that I talk too loud, I overflow and that wears her out.

– MOM!

I looked to see if she was in the yard, sometimes she goes to see and smell the trees in the yard. She stands on the porch and looks at the sky and rubs her forehead. She wasn't there. The bathroom door was closed. I knocked with my elbow because my hands were full.

– Not so loud my God can't you wait a minute?

Her voice is really something else these days. I am never quite sure if she is talking or crying, you might say she swallows her words, you are never sure if the words are coming out or going in.

– What is it, are you sick?

It's silly to ask this question, she is always sick, but then she is never sick. It is her specialty these days and it takes up all her time because she would have to decide once and for all whether or not she is sick and she hates decisions, decisions exhaust her.

– Of course not ... my God ... you're late. The others have already left again.

– Close your eyes before you come out of the bathroom.

It's obvious, I am bothering her. If I disturbed her less, she would probably move even less, maybe she would get to the point of not moving at all. At least that's what I have been thinking lately. You could say that she has no movement coming from the inside anymore, from deep inside. You could say that it is us who are keeping her alive, my brothers and me, because we need to eat and brush our teeth and go to bed. You could say that these are the only things that she is holding onto, at the same time you could say that they are the only things that are holding her together.

I walked around tapping my feet to get on her nerves. I heard water running from the tap. At times she runs the water to wash her hands and then she just stands there listening to it or watching it run. You really have to push her to get her out of it.

– That's enough, come on out now!

All right ...

She turned off the water.

– Wait! Are your eyes closed? Don't open them until I say so.

My brothers didn't notice anything. No one besides me notices because my sisters are in boarding school and besides my sisters there is no one who would really be interested except my father. He notices, but we don't have the same way of noticing. He prefers that those who notice don't talk about it or admit it to each other. That way reactions are freer and there's no need to start a discussion that might turn into an argument, and in any case, you don't know the nature of the virus and maybe there is no virus at all.

She was pale, even paler, and the brown spots on her forehead and temples stood out and she was rubbing the back of her hand. Her hair was dry and flat like after a bad case of the flu and fever and she doesn't like going to the hairdresser, it's too tiring, it takes all her energy for three days and then three days afterwards to get over it. I wondered for a couple of seconds if I should continue worrying about her. When I see her like this, I wonder, I tell myself that it might be better to leave her alone. To be still is what she really wants, what she desires, not to eat, or take baths or to get up anymore, ever, at all.

She did not open her eyes, just as I told her. Maybe she would rather keep them like this because the light hurts her eyes, especially when my father isn't here, when he's gone. She was leaning against the fridge.

STRAWBERRY TIME

– You're home late. Marc and Oliver left for school again a long time ago. It's one o'clock. You only have ten minutes to eat and it's going to be cold, it's already cold.

That's all she could find to say. It was proof of her being a mother and of the good care she gives me. To her, eating cold food is no different than eating hot food. The ideal, for my mom, is not ever to be hungry again, not to ever need to be hungry again in order to live. Her ideal these days is to need sleep in order to live and to sleep all your life to live it.

I put my hands under her nose to see if the smell would wake her up even though I knew she wasn't really sleeping, but I feel better when she is really sleeping than when she is leaning against the fridge like this, rubbing the back of her hand, and you can see those brown spots grow bigger around her eyes and on her forehead.

– Don't you smell anything?

She lifted her head and tried to take three little sniffs of air. It takes all her strength these days. I opened my hands more so it would smell more into her switched-off face. That's it, her face is switched off, and you can't figure out any more how to switch it on, not anybody, not anything, because she has seen lots of doctors and she takes all sorts of medication but she is not switched on.

But now her nostrils were moving and she swallowed and I saw some saliva, just a bit of saliva, between her lips and her lips opened a little more and then she opened up her eyes and said 'Oh.'

It worked. It wasn't exactly the greatest 'oh' you could imagine, but for a person going through a difficult time like my mother, it was quite extraordinary.

Usually she has black eyes, for as long as I can remember she had black eyes and they shone. Then, they stopped shining. It's been about a year. Now, you could say that they're fading, but her hair is still very black without any grey strands here and there. It was with these faded eyes that she looked at my hands and I told her to open her mouth, that I was going to give her the solemn communion of the first strawberries of spring from the end of the world – we are far from everything here and the first strawberries come after everyone else has had them, according to the paper.

– Don't joke around with these kinds of things my God.

She says this because I said 'solemn communion' and she doesn't like it if people are casual about sacred things like communion, which is part of religion and must remain sacred because if you can't tell the difference between what's sacred and what's not, what will become of you, you wouldn't know any longer who you owed what to, or who you owed nothing to because debts are sacred too, my father and my mother are in agreement on this, there is a commandment that says to honour them and there is nothing better than people who honour their debts, you can trust them forever.

Anyways, I put three strawberries on her tongue, the three reddest, the three largest. Her jaws didn't move, I was watching closely, I was watching to see if her tongue would start moving, but nothing moved and she swallowed.

– You swallowed them whole! You could chew them!

– My God oh no how they melt between your tongue and the roof of your mouth.

That's the kind of surprise my mother can give you. You think she's in a coma and then she comes out with a sentence like that, she'll say she likes butter as much as candy or she'll say, 'Did you notice the form of this apple,' you could almost say that an electric current gets the better of her sleep in moments like that. It makes me sweat, I was sweating, this idea that without a single movement of her muscles, she could notice that the strawberries were melting in her mouth and that made me proud of myself. Then her eyes made a sort of inspection of my hands, blouse, jumper and shoes, all without moving her head, nothing but her eyes, slowly, in one go, and she murmured 'strawberries ... '

There, she was off again. Okay. I walked over to the sink, changed my mind and went over to the garbage can and I made the lid slam against the wall.

– Not happy? ... I'll throw them out.

She moved. She unstuck herself from the fridge and stopped rubbing the back of her hand and opened the cupboard and took out a bowl.

– Don't do that, good God, strawberries...

– I haven't had any. See, and there isn't a single stem on them.

It was true. I had not eaten a single one. The patch isn't big. When I saw fat Berubé coming toward me asking if I had found ripe ones, it made me so mad. Every year she thinks that the patch belongs to everybody because it's in a vacant lot and the edges of the roads and ditches are public property. She thinks first-come first-served are just words, she says it every spring each time I find the patch of red berries and it's always me who first thinks of doublechecking these kinds of things and just because she lives two steps from us, she thinks she has the same right to what I see first. 'It is MY patch.' She, Berubé, is perfectly useless in a strawberry patch. She doesn't know how to look she only knows how to squash them with her fat feet, and she only knows how to complain that she can't find anything and how come you find everything it isn't fair. She really gets on my nerves.

My mother squinted, looking out the window over the sink into the yard. I put the strawberries into the bowl. I washed my hands and dried them on the dish towel. It stained the towel red. My mother saw it and sighed. That's the way it is. When she sighs it means she has enough air in her chest for another breath.

– Your lunch is on the table. I am going to lie down a bit. I'll keep the strawberries for my snack. Thanks, sweetheart, they are splendid, splendid.

I repeated it to myself. Splendid, splendid. It's the kind of word she uses for strawberries or pebbles she sometimes finds in the yard. It's a word for everything and nothing, a word to toss off something you don't have, something that really is missing, even though it needn't be.

I wasn't hungry. I looked at my shoes. They are brown. They are Savages, the best for children and adolescents, Monsieur Turgeon who fits us with shoes told my mother that and my mother does not want to buy shoes that are not Savages because Savages are durable too.

I like my shoes. They are scratched just the way I like and really fit my feet without making blisters.

I was already late anyway. A little more or less wouldn't matter, I could take my time. It's like when I know there's a mistake in my dictations, I won't correct it. It's all or nothing with me. If I'm sure there won't be any mistakes, bravo, I correct. But if I know I will make some mistake anyway because there's a word I don't know how to spell, or a verb I don't know how to make agree, then, too bad, I won't correct.

I could hear my mother turn over in her bed even though the door was closed. Before, she used to sing a lot. Now with my brothers at school, it's quiet in our house. Then I heard her cry.

Gerald says that women are made for crying. He says his mother cries for nothing but never he and his dad. He says crying doesn't help anything.

I was careful not to make any noise as I tiptoed up to the door of their room because our floor creaks. It was like I said, I wasn't wrong, she was crying. She cries funny, my mother. First of all, she is not like Gerald's mother, she doesn't cry for nothing, she doesn't ever cry even though her eyes are faded these days and you would think so because of the brown circles around her eyes and on her forehead. She cried once because my sister stepped on a nail and she was the fourth to step on a nail and that meant work and footbaths and lotions. It takes a long time to heal feet, it shouldn't after all you walk with them. But that's the way it is.

That was it all right, she was crying more and more with sobs and sighs. Me, I was on the other side of the door with one hand on the door knob and I asked myself what to do, I was thinking that I should have hurried back to school, after all I had no business here because I'm usually at school at this time and as far as my mother knew I really was at school.

I turned the knob very carefully so she wouldn't jump, scaring her is not what you want to do to someone who thinks she is alone in the house, especially when she is crying and she is sure that no one can hear her.

    I kind of like their room. It is the biggest one in the house. They have a big bed with a dark wooden headboard. On one of the walls, the one where the baby bed is, there is wall paper with white birds on a royal blue background. I don't think my mother will have any more babies, I don't know, but she keeps the baby bed in their room just in case. They have a royal blue down cover on their bed. Now, the royal blue down cover, rising and falling, looked as if it was crying.

    I don't know what's wrong with her. Something must be wrong. It can happen to anyone, something goes wrong and sometimes it lasts a long time, it is solid. I know that. But she is not like everybody. That's my opinion. But what could I do. They each have their dresser and their drawers. She reached out toward her dresser and took the whole box of kleenex with her under the covers. She didn't see me and she could have because of the mirror and she would have jumped because she wouldn't have believed it was me because she doesn't think that I can do anything without making lots of noise or without moving everything including the air.

    I don't know, I left their room, I was too hot. I felt my head to see if I had a temperature because I get fevers for no reason at all and my temples were throbbing. If something could make her temples beat like this, I wonder if she would cry, I don't know.

    I ran. I straightened my jumper and went into class. She had to make some comment, there is nothing I can do without her making a comment. If I wanted her to stop making comments, I would have to be like everyone else here and even then she would find a way to prove to herself that I am like everyone else in order to be different. She says I always find a way to be noticed.

    – You're late, Miss Chavarie.

    That's just like her. That's the way she is, slipping in a comment even if there is no point in disturbing the WHOLE class because ONE student comes in late, since it's obvious that everyone has already seen that anyway. But she always has to make a fuss over something or other.

– You're right, sister, I am late, excuse me for being late, sister.

I must have said it in a special way. Everyone snickered except sister and I. There was nothing funny about it but it is true that I said it in a special way, I agree, she could hold that against me, I'm ready to admit to my mistakes when I make them, I admit them most of the time and when I haven't any, I invent them, I invent even for others if necessary, it doesn't bother me. I opened the top of my desk.

My books and notebooks are all covered with brown wrapping paper, the kind from the Crépeault grocery store, it has a matte side and a shiny side. I put the shiny side out on my books because I think that side is waterproof.

My books were stacked neatly because there had been a general clean-up of our desks seeing that the Department of Public Instruction examination was close and it was a good excuse to clean up. It is beautiful, a desk all in order, because the eyes are the mirror of the soul and because what is clearly conceived comes across clearly. With my head in my desk and the lid on my head, I listened to the silence I had produced in this class. There are many qualities of silence, everybody knows that, I knew that this particular silence was waiting for me to lower the top of my desk because the open top disturbed the whole class, upset the horizontal line of vision that sister needed in order to concentrate because we were in the review period.

I don't know. It was like I was stuck behind this top. It was like I was paralyzed by this lid that I held up with my head while my hands went through my pencil bag for no reason at all. My desk is in the row by the blackboard because in the row by the windows I get too distracted and talk about what is going on outside and I tell the others what's happening in the school yard and who is going down or coming up Second Street and it drives sister crazy to hear me talk about the real world. You can only talk about the outside world the way it's told in the books, for and by the books. The textbook teaches us the colour of the Seine in Paris and its temperature and width and all, and it never talks about the Harricana that cuts right through town here, you cannot talk about that ever ever ever. In any case, this is a colonized country, and that is why you can't start out by knowing the names of the trees and bushes and everything and firetrucks are red anyways like everywhere else, it's international and the earth is bigger than before, when my mother was born the earth was much smaller because mass media was not at the point where it is now, having adjusted the planet to a worldly scale. Anyway, sister had moved my desk to eliminate the distraction. I am sure that the School Board agrees with this decision and I had nothing to say in connection with this.

– Come on, when are you going to come out of your desk?

That's just what I wanted most in this internationalized world – getting to come out of this desk. She could not imagine that, and I wasn't going to tell her the last minute at the end of the school year that we could, she and I, share the same hope even if only for a few seconds. I couldn't do that to her because she would have been too upset at the thought of having been wrong about me for so long. It often happens that I don't correct other people's ideas about me because it's simpler and I figure that everyone else does the same, even to themselves, otherwise we'd be rushed and things would change too fast around us and rapid changes tire most people and give them nausea and migraines and problems.

Well, I felt like crying. I didn't know any more where to turn, I didn't know any more where to hide. I told myself that I had to hold out until four o'clock, that it was absolutely necessary seeing as I was the toughest kid in the whole school and of all the students that sister had ever taught since she started teaching in Nicolet, and from there in Yamachiche, from Yamachiche to La Tuque, from La Tuque to Macamic and from Macamic to Amos and maybe in other towns, I was the toughest, the biggest tomboy, the one with the least heart. I wasn't going to ruin my reputation in two seconds of physical and chemical weakness due to a sudden overproduction by my lachrymal glands. Whatever one says, reputation is made by others through understanding and in opening up of minds and it can go all the way up to the principal of this school where it could be influential. So I clenched and unclenched my jaw, I bit my tongue, I tried to think of the last dirty joke Gerald had told me, I tried hard to find a crazy laugh, nothing.

I lowered the top of my desk because she was coming closer, I just felt it and also I felt that given the tension in the room, there was going to be a hail of gentle rebukes.

She was already next to my desk, I saw her widened nostrils because of the upset, I was sitting and she was standing like a cop who stops a seated driver.

Our eyes met. I saw it in her eyes. The game was won because there was one thing she did not expect at all and she never ever would have imagined me doing such a thing since I really was the one with the least heart and the toughest. I knew that she would lower her eyes as soon as I did it and I did it. I cried right in her face, without letting her go with my eyes or anything and I cried and cried.

So sister was severely punished by this move but I know that something is wrong with my mother and as far as my mother is concerned it doesn't get me anywhere to have someone punished.

Translated by Susanna Finnell.

Stories

Colette Tougas

I want to tell you a story. It's quite simple: it's the story of a woman I have invented to reassure myself when I feel low. It's a bit like a lullaby or a fairy tale for distressed adults, at least for one distressed adult. The reason why this woman is able to reassure me is because she is worse off than I am.

There once was a woman: Clara la Brune was her name. Nobody really knew where she came from, although she said she was a gypsy from Rumania. She came to Paris with her family as a young girl already pregnant and broken-hearted. She was fifteen. Of course, she was pretty, illiterate but intelligent. While her relatives camped on the outskirts of the city trading some thing or other, she spent her days walking. This is how she first met people: she would stroll, then stop in a park, sit and wait for somebody to talk to her; she would just sit there, smile and listen. This is how she learned French. Then winter came and she had her baby — a boy she named Stefan, after her first lover, a German boy with golden hair. Then spring came, and she was on the streets again. This time for good. She met a man who said she could make good money with a face like hers, and money she needed. So she went to live with him, with this man known as Gustave. He owned a café where Clara started entertaining the customers: singing, dancing and doing other things too. Gustave told everyone she was Russian. Clara had told him how her grandmother had met the Czar when she was a young woman, how hot the summer had been, how she was washing her hair in the river, how the Czar thought she was beautiful and made love to her, how her grandmother had a baby, Clara's mother. So Gustave told his customers she was Russian and, just to prove it, he bought her Russian cigarettes to smoke. Every night Clara would open her act with the same song.

CLARA'S SONG

They call me lonely Clara
I'm the lady with a
Russian cigar-a

Some women can kill
Some women can cry
Some women can lie
I'm the one who will
I've gotta move
I know I'm ill
I won't improve
I can't stand still

I live on the sixth floor
And the Fire Department
They're just next door
And from my apartment
I can see their long hoses
Which provokes my attention
I immediately close
All points of observation

My next door neighbour
Cooks pastries all day
It's an earnest labour
And I think he's gay
I hear him sniff and I hear him cry
Cause I know what he makes
He can't help but try
He bakes wedding cakes

They call me Lonely Clara
I'm the lady with a
Russian cigar-a

I could go on and chat
For ages and ages
But you wouldn't like that
I can see you're on edge
Would you prefer to stand
And watch the morning sun?
Come in you'll understand
And we can have some fun

They call me lonely Clara
I'm the lady with a
Russian cigar-a

*

This affair with Gustave lasted a few stormy years, but ended abruptly: one night, an unsatisfied customer came to their room and stabbed Gustave to death. Clara had to hide for awhile. That was easy. She had just met a nice young man, while shopping for a hat.

At this point, everybody thought Clara was ... well, a bit frivolous, but she did not care. All she cared about was that gentle young man, Raoul, who seemed to really love her. They had to meet secretly for Raoul's family would not have approved of this liaison, so he rented an apartment for Clara. This was a very happy time for her. She spent her days inventing songs and stories. She felt young for the first time in her young life. But not for long.

One day, Raoul's father came to her and told her she must stop seeing his son for she was ruining the brilliant career that lay ahead of him in his business. He said she should tell him what kind of a person she really was and leave him. Clara had been expecting this for awhile. She knew she wasn't meant for an easy life because she wasn't like others.

So she wrote Raoul this letter:

Within me there is a fissure that I call the blue hour, through which my shadow escapes, like smoke from a fire. In the twilight of winter days, it slips beyond me to reach the line that separates sky and earth. I am a being of colours; they call me Clara la Brune. The lights of day and night know me better than I know them. My eyes see what I don't understand. My eyes are the guides of my shadow.

I am two. I have the body of a woman and they say it is beautiful, soft, warm skin, black glossy hair. I like touching, eyes closed. This is my body. My eyes open on the light of the times, that is my shadow.

I did not choose this existence, I did not choose my fate, I chose nothing. And yet, I must choose between my body and my shadow, between death in life and life in death. Because day after day, my shadow shows me a shimmering point at the horizon that fear prevents me looking at, but that dazzles my sideways glance.

I run to find refuge within the city walls when I feel my eyes rolling upwards in their orbit. I draw the curtains, I hide in the dark, eyes open. Not seeing anything, eyes open, what a revenge on my shadow which then descends like a fire you put out, back into the cavern of my entrails.

And my insides hurt, and I confuse this pain with desire. And my desire is endless because it is never sated. You see, I am preparing a carnal feast for my shadow; I give it young wildcats, warm, palpitating flesh to savour, but it is never satisfied. No, what it wants, is to fly out of this cage – my body – toward a tiny point on the horizon.

I am writing you this to tell you what danger awaits you, the one I love, it seems. I don't have the courage to leave you ignorant of my identity, and I am tired of fighting an invisible enemy which however lives in the folds of my flesh. Perhaps the hope that you may see it, helped by the distance that I don't have, leads me to confide in you. But if I must admit everything, I must warn you that my shadow delights in this; for the knowledge I am giving you will only stir up the hearth of its wiles as well as of my desire.

Beware of it, my love, and of me.

Clara

By this time Clara had learned that desire and love were two different things and she could not accept this. Why was there so much room inside her, ready to receive somebody's love, if it wasn't meant to be? She could not, did not want to be reasonable about this unfair arrangement, and if she could not find one man to love her, she thought that by having many, she might satisfy her needs.

She was then singing in a nightclub where she enjoyed a particular kind of success that had begun accidentally. One night she had a bad cold and could hardly sing. She decided to tell stories instead. At first the customers were surprised, then they were curious, finally they listened. Clara discovered she had a sense of humour. From that point on, she would intertwine stories and songs in her show.

The stories she told were half-true, but she realized that people actually believed a lot of them. To her surprise, she felt she was having the most intimate relationship she had ever experienced, on a stage, with a hundred men and women listening to her at the same time. There she could invent her past life, glorify it, mythify it and nobody cared because it made them feel good and whole.

Clara would come home at night and think of her childhood; how she was raped by her uncle, let's say; she would tell herself the whole story, the one she remembered and then she would rearrange it. She was not telling lies, just explaining what she felt had happened and why. How many details she had kept inside her memory astounded her: a man's handkerchief, a woman's gesture, the smell of food were still there, intact. Just as the stories reinvented her past, her songs invented her future. The only moment she could call the present came when she was performing for her friends – the audience.

For instance, Clara had always wanted to be rich. So she sang this:

MODESTY

Diamonds around my neck
oh lord they make me chilly
your lips around my neck
oh honey they drive me crazy

*Now I don't want your presents
all I need is your presence*

*A mink coat ain't so hot
oh honey what you've got
makes me wanna purr
to me you're genuine fur*

*Now I don't want presents
all I need is your presence*

*A Rolls-Royce just can't give me
oh lord the ride that you give me
when your engine
is steamin' from too much action*

*Now I don't want your presents
all I need is your presence*

*There ain't no need for gifts
oh I just need you darlin'
but if you insist
I wouldn't mind a few hundred dollars
but it's just to make you happy ...*

Of course, Clara never became rich. The war began, she had to hide because she was a gypsy, then became involved in the Resistance and finally, died alone, poor and bitter, still looking for love.

CLARA'S LAST DAY

Today spring smelt good and warm. I settled myself in the park with the squirrels. I closed my eyes, sitting on a park bench, and went over my life. All the blows I received to my body and my heart have turned me into ground meat. I don't think I have any conscience left.

I still like watching the teenagers hang out after class. They are so clean, well-raised and well-dressed in this part of town. Well-trained animals like at the circus. Come along, little ones, jump through the witch's ring of fire!

That youngster with his straight blond hair and green jacket is handsome as a prince, I said to myself. His appetizing, peachy skin, his eyes bright as fresh water, how I would love to caress that soft warm youth one last time, I said to myself.

I went up to him, offered him the secrets of my race, and took him home with me. I know that my poverty frightened him. Poverty always frightens the rich, just like dirt. I invited him to sit on a saddle set on a stool in the middle of the room that is my home. He really had the look of a horseman, on his imaginary steed. I read the lines on his hand; I lied to him: I foretold him a long and happy life so I could see the dimples appear on his cheeks. As he was a bit cold, I made him an herb tea. He slumped on his imaginary horse. I took him off it, stretched him out on the floor, covered him with a zebra skin. I dressed in my most beautiful fabrics, stolen witnesses of a nomadic past I didn't choose.

He half-woke and I offered him some more tea. I took the teapot over to him to keep him warm. I slipped under the zebra skin and undressed him. I caressed his skin, his flat belly, his blond hairs. I nuzzled his hair, I licked his ears and kissed each one of his eyelashes. He opened his eyes; they were covered with a veil. I drank some of the same tea and undressed. I pressed close to his child's body, warm under the zebra skin.

Now I am waiting for death to come to us. I remember my dark beauty when I look at his blond beauty, and the yellow springtime sun at the window is our only witness.

I was wondering, while writing this, if it was a good idea to tell a story. Stories are strange, because one way or another, they have to make sense. But what they are made of often doesn't. Experiences don't make sense. Wanting to fall in love, meeting new people all the time, getting drunk, working for a living. Nothing really does. But I have an incredible need to put order into this senselessness. It all begins with speaking. The moment I start speaking, I make up stories, I invent an order. I try to create a logic that links up the various elements of a fragment of reality, which in itself is senseless. If somebody asks me: 'What did you do today?' I'll think and then start: 'I got out of bed at 8:00, had breakfast, smoked my first cigarette, packed, took a cab to the train station.' No, no, no. The first thing that happened was that the alarm clock went off, and before the cab, I made a call, and before breakfast, I fed the cats, and before leaving, I got dressed.

All of these things don't make sense separately. Somebody has to worry about them taking place and being integrated into some sort of frame. This is what I'm concerned about. I don't have to be, but I am.

You see, I have to tell you that this Clara la Brune is me. But I don't really live the way I have her live. But if I make sense out of her life, then somehow it works for me.

Another thing I was wondering about concerned the story itself: should I tell you briefly about her whole life or extensively about a small part of it? For example, I could have chosen to retell the time she went to Venice with a friend and there fell in love with a bridge. How she would sit there and look at it at different moments of the day, from various angles, watching the light playing on its surface; imagining all the people who had passed on it since its construction, those who had built it, the others who had carried the stone. How she thought it looked like a good bridge — gentle, strong, useful, handsome.

I don't know, I'm never sure about these things. All I know is I like stories.

128 Park Avenue

Hélène Le Beau

Her name is ... it doesn't really matter, especially in the mornings. Obviously when she comes home in the evenings and imagines someone calling her by her name, Jeanne, Lucette or Carmen, it's not the same thing. But nobody calls her Jeanne or Lucette or Carmen, and certainly not 'sweetheart' when she gets home in the evening; if anyone calls her name at all, it's an indefinable 'Mmmom', always the same 'Hey, Mmmom, what's there to eat, Mmmom?'

Mmmom, or Jeanne or Lucette or Carmen, with her hair not done, it's not important in the winter under her polyester hat from Woolworth's, takes the 128 Park Avenue bus every morning at 8:23. She goes downtown. Every morning, because she gets on at the corner of Fairmount and Park, there's no room on the bus, even if she sees the excited bunch of kids from the College Français get off, even if she always manages to be first in line, the bus is full; she'd have to walk as far as Outremont to get a seat or look so tired, so discouraged, that some guy, not too engrossed in his newspaper, and not too young either would offer her his seat, all the while telling himself that next time he'd pretend not to see her. Mmmom remembers the day a man offered her his seat. It was the guy who was always reading Montréal-Matin. She'd been grateful. She'd also made sure for a long time after to be anywhere else in that bus except in the man's field of vision for fear he would offer her his seat again. Nice people like that have to be handled considerately, and she knows it bothered him; she doesn't like to bother people, Mmmom doesn't.

The driver knows her. He knows everybody, even though he asks the regulars often enough to show their passes and pretends not to have seen them before. It's his way of making conversation.

'Move along to the back!' She feels hot; she always feels hot; the others too. Winter or summer, all the time, it's hot, except for the people seated next to the windows as if to prevent the ones that are hot from opening them. Madame Mmmom sees the same faces, the weariness, the Fort Lauderdale suntans she'd never dare to get because she feels so fat and ugly, too old for the beach, for taking walks, for the pool.

Her shoes, shoved into the bag her sister-in-law gave her for Christmas last year, the only time she ever gave her a present, probably because Maurice died the week before, get crushed a bit more every morning, when she lets people by who absolutely have to go through to the back even though there's no more room there. She finds the back noisy and dirty and she feels as though everyone is looking at her, and the comfort of the people who have seats makes her feel as aggressive as Stevie does, when he's lying in front of the T.V. shouting 'Hey ...'.

People are all the same. 'Hey, Missus ... what's the special?' The special is the tip, mister, a good tip for the fries that aren't too greasy, the coffee that's not too weak, for the time she saves him because she's quick; she doesn't smile, that's true, but her legs are so sore, her fat, ugly, old legs she has such a hard time seeing sometimes in the morning when she stands on the chair in the entrance and looks at them in the mirror. Because in the restaurant she runs all the time; she does so much running she just has time enough, five minutes at the most, to eat a grilled cheese sandwich at the corner of the table at the back near the kitchen; in any case she doesn't really have the right, except if she pays half-price for the special without the soup, or the beverage, or anything else. Because her boss is a cheap bastard who started out with souvlakis and ended up in continental cuisine. His memory of the time when he was washing dishes is too fresh for him not to treat his employees the same. That's why she doesn't leave her shoes at work either, he'd be crazy enough to throw them out.

So she drags them along in the bag, already torn, the one her sister-in-law gave her the other Christmas, even though she does crush them a bit more every day because she insists on staying where she is, stubbornly in the passage; she won't ever go to the back. Her standing, and the others sitting, no thank you. It's still better crowded into the middle. At least if she feels sick, she can breathe when the doors open, move a bit to pretend to be getting off.

On the hill at Bleury, the other side of Sherbrooke, when everybody gets up to catch the métro, she's always scared. Because once she was pushed around so much, she had to get off and take the next 128. That was when the passes didn't exist yet. She was so afraid the driver wouldn't believe her story about being carried off by a wave of rushing people (that is just how she felt, like a jellyfish picked up from the edge of the sea by a wave and thrown back on the sand, sometimes she even says she liked the feeling), that she paid again and didn't use her transfer or her head, her messy Wednesday-morning head.

So, on the hill, she tries to slip through between the impatient passengers like a salmon fighting the current upstream, and with a bit of luck she finds a seat before the bus crosses Ontario Street. This is the only rest she has all day, two stops, only two stops, without her shoes getting crushed or anything else. Nothing except the people getting off. Now she closes her eyes, and this is the only moment of the day she thinks of Stevie with a tenderness she won't feel again until tomorrow. She doesn't think about her pay, or her tips, or the customers, or about Maurice and his cancer, or about the unshaven man who looks like her father and who she sees on the bus home at quarter past five every night (she stands in this bus too; if she sits down her legs fall asleep and she's sure she won't be able to get up again, ever, or only at stops much farther along, too far to get home in time to prepare Stevie's supper), and she doesn't think either about the dreams she sometimes has about having her man with her in a big bed of waves, again those waves, like he promised, telling her she has the most beautiful legs in the world with a Fort Lauderdale tan right up to her neck, her ears, a sunshine smile on her fat, ugly, old body.

She doesn't think. She just lets the silence invade her, a silence with no demands, no orders. Two stops: St. Catherine, Dorchester. In this short moment that is hers, she imagines herself dying four thousand times, asleep on her bus seat, without anyone noticing her fat, ugly, old body endlessly travelling back and forth on the 128 Park Avenue bus, cutting the city in two with its perpetual journeys, and them leaving her there because they couldn't give a damn, the rushing crowds, the excited kids, the poor, the school children, the drivers taking over from each other, all of them with nothing to do but forget her, leaving her there with her crushed shoes in her bag on her lap.

Henna for Luck

Madeleine Ouellette-Michalska

Right in the middle of the dance floor, Slimane was dancing alone. His head pressed into empty space, he held himself upright, one leg supporting his slender body below the darkness of the ceiling. The moment of support between steps was so short that the two leaps melted into the single throb of a meticulous *chassé*, executed beyond thought and space, only by the thrust of instinct, or of delirium – this was the impression of some of the onlookers watching the big black bird locked in a ferocious battle with the ground, its delicate frame ceaselessly wrenching itself away, trying to free itself and keeping them all cowering in anxiety – the two Vikings, the Saint Bernard, Genevieve, Barbara and the others, all those who knew the story and were expecting the worst.

Slimane was relieved of the waiting and the fear. He continued dancing, apparently effortlessly keeping time with the charleston which had risen to fever pitch, threatening to suffocate the audience unable to endure the frenzied passion any longer, the convulsive fury that recalled the spell-binding trances of firebreathers. Everyone was watching him, filled with consternation mixed with fear and pity. Would the scene continue to unfold, or would it end, leaving them with a skeleton they wouldn't know what to do with, a livid body with a haggard, crazed head, detached from the music and rolling at their feet, that would return to haunt them at night?

They couldn't forget Slimane's silhouette leaping from rock to rock, his dark eyes suddenly becoming glassy, his animal cry echoed by the mountain, his silence, and finally his unrestrained grief. They recalled his body lying next to the young girl's, their heads tipped back in the murderous sunlight, their legs bent and lapped by the indifferent waves. Round about nothing had changed. There was the foam splattering the cliff, the crowd of bathers running and shouting amid the parasols stuck into the burning sand, the rounds of the watermelon sellers, the absurd silence of the sky, the fishing boats moored as before, as always since the beginning of summer.

Into this shimmering light and distant hum, Slimane's sudden awakening. They couldn't wipe away the memory of the boy's arms encircling the girl urging her to get up, his perseverance, his relentless repetition of a name she remained deaf to. Fadila! Fadila! She no longer saw the sky, or the sea, or anyone. She didn't feel the hands that caressed her, touching her ears, her mouth, her cheeks, and suddenly freezing at the left temple.

Slimane's fingers were stained with an accursed blood that no salvo of shots would acclaim in the rituals of defloration. The bridegroom would not be led in triumph from the nuptial chamber to join the men. The women would not cry behind the partitions and would not give way to excessive rejoicing. They would not snatch for the nightdress to check the signs, still warm, of conquered virginity. They would search in vain under Fadila's pillow for the tiny knife and the mirror set in silver.

Beauty and audacity had escaped the rites of the tribe. They lay at the foot of the cliff, accusing, forming an unbearable stain of light. The onlookers shivered in spite of the heat. They moved away softly, overwhelmed by the inevitable that no derisive comment could reduce to chance.

'It's incredible!' said the Saint Bernard.

Genevieve shared this opinion and added, ' It's absurd.'

Slimane heard nothing.

He was dancing, sweat streaming down his forehead. The men had begun to clap their hands. Their applause stressed the rhythm, splintering it into motifs that rebounded between the boy's legs forcing him to move even faster. Fadila's steps took shape between his. They crunched the gravel along the edge of the road, shook the noontime torpor, drowned out the lapping of the waves and the droning of the cars.

One of the cars stopped, ready to seize the prey slipping away into the light. The young woman plunged down the bank and disappeared into the brush, fleeing the cliff road and the ambushes awaiting her there. 'Where are you going?' 'You want to come for a ride?' 'Get in, or I'll take you home to your father!' She took a path already trodden by goats, readjusted her headscarf and did up the overcoat that covered her white arms, her pink gandoura, her golden jewellry. Her charms were well protected. She would be able to defend them against any violation.

She was almost running, resolved to take the fate she'd been deprived of into her own hands. She would hold it for only a second, and no one would be able to stop her, not even the man taking part in the offensive festivities. The cicadas' song had become too shrill. This strident summer noise was as exhausting as running in the sun. Fadila slumped under a tree and examined the area to make sure she was alone.

Reassured, she leaned her head against the tree and closed her eyes. Rid of onlookers, she felt more clearly the life pulsing within her. This flight contrasted with habits of languour and ease. She heard the sea nearby, its cradling rhythm. And words came back to her, inexhaustible like her pain.

'Fadila, you're the most beautiful girl I know.'
'Say it again.'
'You're the most beautiful woman of all.'

Two ardent eyes were resting on her. Pressed to Slimane, she matched his passion, and dreaded his demands and fits of rage.

'Will you always love me?'
'I'll love you as long as there are stars.'
'Here, you don't marry who you want.'
He shushed her.

They had been able to choose, others would do the same. She let herself be convinced, more sensitive to reasons of the flesh than to the force of the argument. This love, that sometimes took the form of combat, brought her the feeling of a definitive power, the knowledge of a superior state that others envied them for. She loved the gentleness of their relations, but also the violent confrontations that pitted them one against the other until their lips drew close in the same uneasy surge.

Exhausted, Fadila brushed at the mosquitoes on her face while Slimane continued dancing. As soon as she felt the thrust shake the boy's body, she got up, put on her coat and covered her hair. He leapt up, amassing shadow around his shoulders while she rushed out into the blinding light, propelled by a rhythm as demanding as the orchestra's. Her hands lifted her skirt off the tufts of broom and smoothed it down over her knees in two silky panels that swished under the stiff fabric of the coat.

She was running, skirting the narrow bays between the rocks and climbing up the cliff grasping onto the roots of the scorched cedars. She avoided looking at the light sand of the shore, the clusters of mimosa in bloom, the slow swell that licked the beach. She distrusted the gentleness of the landscape. To strengthen her resolve she revived the anger that had possessed her for two weeks. Two weeks of fury during which she had at first collapsed in despair, wallowed in laments, then had straightened up, resolved and complete. It was six o'clock in the evening. A sudden determination had come over her; at first she'd considered it coldly, then accepted it as irremediable.

The bay was dipping its bright belly into the sea. She looked out beyond the last rock into the cove where the waves were breaking on the stones. Fadila recalled the broken rock at this spot, its points biting into the sky, the unyielding violence of its spurs and crests. She found its rugged shape again, located the narrow gorge between the escarpments into which she had followed Slimane who was pulling her forward crying, 'Don't leave me!' They were trampling down a patch of red grass. She was clinging to him, torn between two attractions. The immense, roaring sea behind her, beating the invisible earth. Him in front, laughing, his face almost white. She understood his desire to open her savagely on this patch of grass, and his wish, equally strong, to keep her intact for the approaching wedding night.

Somber, almost tragic, the bridegroom was distractedly receiving good wishes. 'May you have a long life, Slimane!' 'We wish you a boy as your first-born!' 'May the blessings of Allah accompany you to the end of your days!' Allah and the lineage were a single branch, an indestructible tree to which he had just become attached. The country was swarming with children, yet they wanted more. The midwives were never done cutting the umbilical cords of the newborn, and the circumcision rituals mingled their scraps of dead flesh with the putrified bodies piled in the ancestral gardens. The chainlinking of the sexes created a kingdom of males, but life relentlessly devoured what the women's bodies strained to produce.

Before he went to fetch his bride from her home, a baby had been laid into her arms to ensure her fertility. The old women whispering in the corners assessed the bride's chances and found her hips narrow, her chest hollow. Oh Fadila, so beautiful and complete in her shapely curves! Fadila, so happy in her body and soul! Fadila, languishing in the sun and revived at night by the scent of jasmin, where was she? Why was she not a part of these brilliant ceremonies?

She was approaching, touching the rock whose dry grain she recognized, its spurs jutting sharply into empty space. She stepped back, examined the islet of red grass, and then stretched out alone in the shadowy groove that fitted her body perfectly. But music exploded in her head and made a long shiver run down her body. She got up, came back into the sunlight, took off her coat, her shoes, her golden belt. The gandoura billowed out. Breathless, Fadila undid the scarf that held her hair and tilting her head made the shimmering mass fall over her forehead. She moved to the outermost point of the rock, seeing nothing but hair and the foamy crests of the breakers far below.

A cry escaped from the bridegroom's throat and he refused to dance any longer. But they forced him to continue, dragging him out in front of the orchestra. For the benefit of the males, he was to roll his hips and display his body, perform the gesture of solitary pleasure and prolong the ritual intoxication. The tribe required this spectacle and demanded these pleasures as a distraction from the gloom of daily life. 'Dance, Slimane!' And the orchestra scraped its strings and beat its drums drawing out the harsh and nasal sabre dance below the ballroom ceiling. Slimane, a false Tuareg, slashed the space with large blows, his left foot slipping on the tiles, his right bracing itself against the thrust of the knife.

His mother drew back, livid.

'Slimane, you don't have the right!'

He moved forward threateningly, his arms reducing the distance between him and the woman. 'You'll be damned!' Before the hell opening up, the prohibitions and the power of the clan, he was yielding and consenting to incest. He bent in front of the woman who was taking Fadila away from him and imposing her niece, a thin girl he'd seen only occasionally at funerals. Thus the blood-line would not suffer division. It would return to the tribe just as the Rummel had been flowing into the sea for centuries.

The celebration was continuing, carried along by the music that beat out the rhythm of the festivities. People gorged themselves on kebabs, couscous, honey cakes and almonds. The women bustled about showing off their clothes and jewels. In a separate group, the men regaled themselves with rampant lechery. The rejoicing would continue for seven days. Then the clamp would snap down on the couple, and Slimane would be bored for the rest of his life. This evening he would join the bride, and in the shadows of the bedroom, his arms would welcome a stranger who would reawaken his hatred for his mother.

His heart stayed cold, attached to Fadila who was running and knocking on neighbours' doors.

'If I've ever offended you, please forgive me.'

Frightened, the women immediately closed their doors. They hid behind the shutters and watched the child who was doomed to the Prophet's curse disappear.

Fadila went back up the street, crossed the square without looking back, skirted Sidi Benmalek's newspaper stand, and climbed the steps that led to the baths. She entered, paying the matron, and crossing through the empty and silent main bath, she went to the room reserved for brides. In the alcove she undid her hair, took off her dress and wearily looked at her body. It was virgin, as intact as the day she was born. No one had really touched it, not even Slimane who had promised to marry it.

Wrapping herself in a towel, she approached the water and sank slowly into it. Air bubbles formed around her. She burst them one by one surrounding herself with total emptiness before she lathered her body with soap. The water slipped between her breasts and ran down her flat belly, waking a great sadness in her. She twisted her hair, and floated on her back in the foam forcing herself to think of nothing. New bubbles appeared; she burst them in a state of dizzy exhaustion. Time congealed. She managed to forget who she was and why she'd come to the baths.

The matron was getting impatient. Fadila had to get out of the water and dry off. They gave her oil and powder and perfume. They rubbed her feet and hands with 'Henna for blissful nights', as the label on the bottle promised. She put on the velvet gandoura, bedecked herself with her jewels, and did her hair. She brushed her eyebrows and edged her eyes with khol. An empty face gazed back from the mirror they held for her.

She cast a quick glance at this forbidden beauty she was no longer consciously inhabiting and got up. She had to leave the reassuring shade of the baths, forget the steaming heat that had soothed her. She had to go out to confront the sun and exorcise her fear. The old woman's admiring glance followed her, confirming her status as a desirable creature. She lowered her eyes.

Abruptly the bridegroom reared up and tore himself out of the rhythm that was making his body sway continuously. He regained his balance, reducing the spasms that continued to shake his hips after his torso had already stopped moving. Men surrounded him. He broke through the group and rushed to the exit.

Outside, the heat was torrid. He turned his back to the sun and looked at the sea. This liquid opening made him shiver. He leaned against the freshly whitewashed garden gates and vomited. Then he raised his head. Without turning back, he went through the gateway scented with mint, determined to get away.

A cry rose from the far point of the cliff. He began to run in the direction of the cry. His instinct told him which shortcuts to take, which crevasses to avoid. It led him straight to his goal, the far point of the headland where the coast closes on an eddy pulled in by the breakers.

Below, the light fell on a rock spattered with blood. A second, final cry rose. The man fell to the ground, collapsed in pain. He lay moaning before the people fascinated by the horror.

'Did it last a long time?'

'A good half hour.'

'Have the mourners come?'

'No. Tomorrow they'll go to the girl's parents.'

'Have the police been notified?'

'Probably, we didn't stay till the end.'

'It's unbelievable.'

Genevieve was repeating it a second time. Barbara took no notice; neither did the two Vikings and the big Saint Bernard. Seated at their usual table, they sipped their whisky bewitched by the dancer.

No one else was on the dance floor. All alone, Slimane was grinding up the space, his face an expression of unbearable fury. Convulsions rattled his torso, delivering up his body to frenzied distortion. The pain was violent, spellbinding.

'Do you think he's lost his mind?'

'Very likely.'

Tenderness

Marie-Claire Blais

They were sleeping together, gently entwined. They had known each other for only a few hours, had only exchanged a few words, a few brief caresses, and yet the room was full of them, full of the sensual relationship of their bodies and of their lives come to warm up near one another on this cold March night. Outside, an icy spring deluge could be heard, the smell of rain and fog still permeated their clothes, the too heavy coats, the muddy shoes, things that had suddenly become dismal necessities, when they entered the apartment and which they had strewn about them in the ardour of their invading senses. Now they were sleeping or pretending to sleep, their gaze, their hands, still reaching out for each other in the warm refuge of the bed. The surge of sudden tenderness, but also their nervousness at the sexual encounter, their first embrace in the night, had surprised them, as they lay intertwined in this uncharted oasis. Wasn't it perhaps, they surmised, nothing more than a friendly, virginal encounter, doesn't the drab light of dawn often erase the luminous gestures of the night, would not each of them in the morning respond to life's inexorable duties?

Soon the dazzling summer would be upon them, why should they leave each other already, so soon, and under their drowzy eyelids, their gaze awoke, both anxious and ardent, the summer light was already drawing them together, their cheeks were burning, their eyes sparkling at this fleeting hope, life, summer, us, this frantic moment of love held within a room, in the knowledge that beyond, there will soon be only cold and alienation. One of them wondered what it was that she liked so much about the other, was it the thick strand of hair that hung over her long ear or her small solid foot, so muscular that it seemed all set for running – but was it for running or for running away? – this foot she had held deliciously in her hand? But she also felt that in this wild field that the night had revealed to her, everything about the body of the other was familiar, from the salty tears at the corner of her eyes, whose flavour she knew, for at the rim of the other's eyes is her soul, suddenly cautious, vigilant, which had leaned over her, suspending the body's ecstasy (and she had thought: she has just come into me with no hesitation, I will love her, how can I help it?) from her suppressed tears to the strength of her narrow foot, which had made her smile, every one of these details of a body joyously explored, didn't it hold you in painful closeness, for you had to know everything, at least understand everything about this supreme disorder that was bursting into your life.

The other was feeling cold perhaps, or did she have a premonition of an imminent leave-taking, she said, 'Cover your shoulders', as though she had always talked to her like that, murmuring in a low voice, but in a subtly imperious tone, giving an order to the one she was already obscurely calling my girlfriend. But the thoughtfulness of these words, these gestures, could also be shown other lovers over the course of many nights. And she who had pressed her lips on the wrinkle that lined the other's cheek, who had tasted the bitterness of her tears, felt the fragments of earlier lives pass between them, these fragments that seethed alone or in complete isolation, in the sensuous air of the room. It was suddenly cold since the other was covering her breast with a sportshirt, concealing the beauty of a child's torso (where she had just been talking about the deterioration that is a part of all life, along with suffering and time) and these words were still floating in the room, with their grave modesty, the splintering of the splendid days they had sheltered, this thing, a piece of blue cotton which the other's body had draped around itself, shivering with cold, this thing became in the first glimmer of dawn, the flesh and scent of the other, bearing all her imprints. The blue cotton shirt with its short sleeves, frayed as though the other's impatient hands had hacked them off (and those yellow reflections under the armpits, or rather a yellow transparence, for the down of the armpits could be seen brown underneath, as though below the blaze of this body there were other fires smouldering, peaceful, dormant, clothing having the sole purpose of subjecting them to the laws of a cold season), this piece of pale-blue clothing which the dawn light revealed, was breathing in harmony with the other's breast, listening as the ear of a lover would, to the beating of her heart. Instead of enveloping the one who was cold in its blue raggedness, it suddenly uncovered her, revealing a succession of charms, the belly muscles where one could rest one's head, despite their hardness, the strong thighs that led to the intrepid feet, so willful in their urge to leave, to move, that the passionate fingers could no longer calm them, letting them amuse themselves in pursuit of their dreams or their anxious agitation, for isn't the body like the rest of us, complicated, obstinate, with a stubbornness that expresses the ascent toward a liberty so delicately restrained?

Suddenly into this violent day, came a morning of extreme violence since with its gray light, its cold wind that had blown down trees during the night, it separated these hands that were still so warm and now avoided meeting, suddenly, it was time to leave, but their eyes still held the same hope as when they had slept in each other's arms, all the while not sleeping, and watching their desires through half-open eyes, the hope they didn't talk about while they accepted everything, this superabundance of sudden gifts that dizzied them, the hope that was hardly anything and perhaps everything, more love, love tomorrow, perhaps, for the moment, the memory of their double breathing in the night.

The Story of

Lori Saint-Martin

I

At fifteen my first suicide attempt failed. The second one weaves itself gently in the dark. Exploration and slow insomnia. Defer it until the right moment. A story not worth finishing. I will live?

II

Transform into violence this good girl's face. Hate and lipstick; anger and mascara. At fifteen the equivalences are clear.

III

Even though I have gazed at myself in the mirror to the point of nausea I don't possess a single one of my features. 'I' slips from my hands, is good for nothing.

IV

Rage, desire. No cry. Don't wake the sleeping mother. Savour the ambiguity for an instant yet. Hardly sketched bodies I wanted.

Fifteen years. I looked for you. Heaviness, breakage. Panting. Wanted, this time, finally I wanted something, to save myself. Your profile founders on the backgound of the wall.

But already you are telling about your friends looking for girls. You say: a girl like you. To make me understand that it's nothing really, but that we're necessary, girls like me, like me.

V

Every afternoon my sister devours my diary entries of the night before. My mother waits for news bulletins from the front. I don't know anymore if I am writing for her or not.

VI

Fifteen years. On the doorstep, my father: look like a damned slut, you, still. Takes off his belt. Me. The neighbour women, the boys. It is summer, they see, it's deliberate, the game has these splinters.

Who should be punished?

Once beyond the door, I hang around the streets, a wound in my secret blood. One man, another, nothing heals, the silence thickens, strangles itself. Never want to go home. Or think about. Behind the door, they're waiting for me, not talking. Raise their hands again and again against me.

VII

'You can always tell when a girl has been with a man.' I go back, softly, littlegirlly. Hide the moisture. If there is some deliverance in it, it is not for me.

I am the blood stain on the burnt sheet, the half-open door through which the life murmurs pass.

VIII

My mother cries, furious, her hands in the dirty dishwater. Does not wipe off her tears her tears are for me. My own rage fills me what souring mama I don't want to see anything.

Your pain is not equal to my contempt for you two mama if I insist on this rage it is perhaps because I am fighting. And still I have not found a single reason for living in this garish summer, these alleys, in the shadow of all these bodies.

IX

... full of consequences. We grow quieter without believing in it. My father has become a gentle man. Hard to believe that. Still it is the same man.

My mother is still waiting. Makes beds, washes windows, writes me: it is mild, we've had rain, we planted the garden. Not a word from my father. Sometimes his voice on the telephone, polite. Paper frightens him.

X

Where does this wretched calm come from? Quietly a woman weaves in the dark. I am still fifteen. The cry / the voice / the door always the door.

It Would Be Night

Claire Dé

First, it would be night. The man would be stretched out naked under the quilt, and it would be night. The man would seem to be sleeping but he would be waiting. At the agreed time someone would have rung. A gloved hand would have rung, ten stories below. He would know. He would have seen himself hesitate before answering, but would still answer. A moment ago. Hardly three minutes ago. A century.

It would be night. A Tuesday or Wednesday, an unimportant day of the week. It would have snowed. Late yesterday, also in the night, he would have phoned the woman. He would only have said:

It's me.

She would have replied:

I know. When?

Midnight tomorrow.

Midnight. Tonight. Right away.

Perhaps she won't come. She would have taken the elevator, gone up but then down again. She too would have hesitated. She would have been afraid of the man. Or of herself. Still she would have said When? with such assurance. As though she knew that he would call. As though she'd been thinking about him, just when he picked up the phone.

It would be night. The man's heart would be aching, a little like it had when he was so unhappy he couldn't bear to live any longer. Would it be a dream? Magic? Impossible? Illegal? His heart would be pounding, but differently. His heart would be dancing. From fear. And from happiness too.

The door would have opened, then clapped like thunder in the quiet studio. In the dark, his eyes shut, the man would have smiled. Why does this woman, so fragile, always slam doors so vehemently? From what kind of prison ... ?

The woman would have entered the studio. She would have walked silently past the bay window, keeping on her fur. In the dark, the man stretched out in the bed would not have seen her, he would have smelt her. A mixture of ylang-ylang and wild cat. The cognac he'd poured her would glow in its glass on the table.

She would have sipped it slowly, still walking. With her gloves still on, he'd know that too. Chloe. He would hardly remember her last name, but suddenly recall the scent of her perfume. The pungent ylang-ylang freshened with a tip of jasmin.

Memories, in breaths of Chloe, would have whirled in the man's head with her scent, the beauty mark above her lips, the taste of her hair at the nape of her neck, her cream cheese skin. Her sex.

It would be night. The last time she'd said: I want you. A husky, throaty I want you. The last time. She would so have liked there to be no last time. The last time, so long ago. The last time.

Each time they met, each time she would have been afraid it was the last time: she knew this man would always elude her. She would have said I want you.

I want you because one night you held my wrist in your hand. Didn't clutch it, or grip it, just held it, and she would think that his hand decorated her wrist like the loveliest of bracelets. I want you because your kisses, your caresses, you, leave my skin luminescent. Because when you love me, I am beautiful, I no longer walk, I am a dancing serpent. I want you because. I want what you want. Deliver you from your fears. Tame your suffering. I dream what you dream. I am here. For you.

It would be night. She would only have said: I want you, in a husky voice. He would remember this I want you, now that she would be there, pacing silently in front of the bay window. Sipping her cognac, and exuding the ylang-ylang and wild cat scent. Then

IT WOULD BE NIGHT

she would have put the empty glass on the table. Taken off her gloves. Abruptly opened the curtains.

It would be night. The man would seem to be sleeping, but he'd be waiting. The woman in her lynx coat would be pressed against the window. Legs apart, arms crossed. A shadow over the scattered lights of the city.

She would have shivered, and said I'm cold, but a different trembling would tingle her skin. The waiting, the desire. From the tenth floor she would have gazed at the city in its nocturnal case, like a queen contemplating her jewels, yet never would a queen have been more adorned than she was that night, since he would be giving himself to her, and she herself to him.

It would be night. The woman would have turned toward him, letting her fur coat slip off. The man would have started. She would be naked, already naked, he wouldn't have seen her, his eyes would still be closed. No, he would have smelt her. Her woman smell would have swept through the studio in one gust, beyond her Chloe, beyond his own smell.

The man would finally have opened his eyes, she would be there, standing in front of him, close, naked. She would be looking at him too, her eyes shining in the dark. The satin of tears. The lustre of desire too.

The man, stretched out and naked under the quilt, would not move. He would seem to be sleeping with his eyes open. He would have closed them again when the woman slipped in beside him. For a long time they would have stayed like that, skin to skin, listening to the other's breathing. Their skin would have burnt them and would burn them still. Especially her, come in from the cold, naked under her coat.

They would resemble each other, the same delicate joints, the same matte skin, brown hair. But he would be solid, strong, while she was slender, her belly flat, her breasts small, as though she'd refused to grow up. She would be smaller than he, to reach his lips she would have had to stretch, tauten her throat. His caresses, him, his sex would fulfill her so.

It would be night. Neither one of them would have moved. Then the man would have sighed like a child in its sleep, and nestled his face into the woman's neck. Her arm would have slid around his waist, his around her shoulders. Closer still. Gently close, closer, like coming out of a dream.

She would have been dreaming of a black stallion prancing in front of her, mane flowing, nostrils steaming, coming up to her and tearing her dress into shreds, into petals, he would have fed on her, grazed on her. Then she would have straddled him and galloped off headlong across a never-ending plain.

It would be night. The studio would be warm. Stretched out under the quilt, naked, side by side, the man and the woman would have caressed each other's backs, that distant, ever uncharted continent.

It would be night. With the implacable gentleness of woman, the gentleness of maple syrup and honey, the gentleness of damp, intrusive moss, the woman would have held him still tighter, pressed against him. They would have rolled over, she lifting herself onto him, feet to feet, knees to knees, thighs to thighs, breasts to chest, tensed belly to erect sex.

Only then would she have touched his lips with hers, gently biting them, plump, succulent lips, she would have seemed to him to have thirsted to death for centuries from not having drunk of his water. Imperceptibly she would have grown dizzy from head to foot. The man, his eyes closed, would have noticed, while their hands would suddenly have run riot over their bodies.

It would be night. The man and the woman would not be sleeping, they would be locked in an embrace, floating, entranced. Tireless caresses and kisses. Then he would have tried to put his hand there, she would have moved away, while her hand would have seized him, and held him firmly. Kissing him she would have said:

Ask me to take you in my mouth.

Take me in your mouth the man would have said. What a strange smile she would have had then. He couldn't know her obsession, the fixed purpose of her solitary dreams, that he spill himself into her throat. That he be absolutely in her possession, for once. That he abandon himself.

He would have been one of the many men who caress themselves, so tight and fast, no vagina, no mouth can compete with their rapid thrust. She would have liked him to learn the pleasure of letting her have her way with him.

It would be night. He couldn't know that she has kissed his photo so often that no longer black and white, it has turned crimson from her lipstick. This man, this man's presence would raise a violent wind within her, a strange firewind that would seize her, exhilarate her. It would all seem so simple and complicated to her, so fragile and strong, and so delicious. Why this feeling of eternity at the same time as the acid bite of the dying present?

It would be night. In the dark the man wouldn't see the woman's face clearly. She would have reached up, wedged the firm pillow under his hips and disappeared under the quilt. The man would not be sleeping, he would be waiting, and perhaps a luscious agony would have made him tremble, his fingers would have tangled in the woman's hair, the woman, the woman's mouth would have come, moistened him, licking, lingering, moving to the inner thigh, returning, his whole being would be throbbing there, in his center, then she would open her lips on the nub, close them over its verge.

It would be night. Now he would be pushing against her, but her head would have gone up and down, inexorable. His turn now to say I want you. I want you, but she would only make him plunge deeper into her throat, he would have become a burning ecstasy, his whole being tensed, arched, the climax massing within him, quickening, he chokes, explodes. Comes.

It would be night. The quilt would have slipped to the ground. The man would not be sleeping, he would be coming back to himself, to the world, to the dark studio, to the light spangles of the city in the bay window, he would have come back to himself and to the woman, who would seem to be sleeping, her cheek against his sex.

But she wouldn't be asleep, she would have sat up, stretched, she would be laughing softly, running her hands over his chest.

Then she would have leant against the head of the bed, thoughtful. She would have lowered her eyes and raised one thigh. Moved her fingers into the lips of her sex. He would not be dreaming, she would have caressed herself in front of him, beside him, silently, as though not to disturb anyone. He would see her rise up and quiver like a wave, see her fingers pull her lips upward, he would see her forefinger fluttering. She would open wide like a flower in the sun, the man would be erect again. The woman would be on the point of climax, she would have tipped her head back, her sighs would have deepened, her nostrils dilated, her mouth opened to cry but she doesn't cry, she comes. Implodes. Storms.

It would be night. For a long time the man would have leant over the woman, a small creature, dead or passed out. But she wouldn't be dead or passed out, and she wouldn't be sleeping either, she would open glistening eyes and contemplate him leaning over her, his erection. Her desire for him suddenly so strong, she would reach out for him, seek his body, his lips.

The man and the woman would have embraced like two fighters, and would be struggling. You win, you win, the man would finally have said, his shoulders pinned to the mattress.

Wait, the woman would say.

She would take a phial of light oil from the bedside table, she would pour a little into her palm, then rub it into his skin.

It would be night. The man would not be sleeping, he would moan softly, the woman caressing him with both hands, his hand searching for her breasts, a hip, her sex, rubbing against his leg. Then, suddenly she would straddle him. Long and terrible moment of suspended, trembling desire. She would be breathless, merged with him, flesh sizzling before meltdown, both root and ocean, before the surge, with its crests and its hollows where they would catch their breath, its backwash and swells, salty kisses and seaweed caresses.

IT WOULD BE NIGHT

It would be night. The man would not be able to sustain this extended immobility, and still fused to her he would have rolled her under him, he would no longer know if it were her drawing him in, or him grinding into her, she would forget herself, he would forget himself, he would crush her, she bite him, they would be reeling, rolling, she would clamp her feet around his hips, the animal love machine catches, opens, contracts, thrusts, sways, roars, a crazy dance, she would feel him swelling, still hardening, within her too it would be rising, boiling, wanting an escape, she would be growling, he groaning, the end of the rush, peaking, the explosion cuts through them, swallows them up. Consumes them. Climax.

He would have told her:
It's me.
She would have said:
When?
She would have said When? so often, before. When are you coming back? Don't you know my heart would be lighter if I knew When? All this When? from the neglected lover. The last time it was winter too, she hadn't said When? The last time, when he'd pulled away from her, she'd let out the sob of a doe at bay. A single blow, distance. She'd bounded to her feet, gone for the cigarettes to keep him naked by her side a little longer. She'd rested her head on the man's chest, a long moment that was too short. He'd sighed like someone who has to leave, she'd pointed it out to him. He was surprised that she'd guessed. And soon, he'd gone. She'd pressed her cheek and her body against the frosted window. Melting, the frost had pearled her with icy tears.

It would be night. She and he, caught in the noose of fate, shaped from solitude, silence and desires. I can see what could have been and what will never be. I was madly in love with you, you left me. Since then, it is always night. Yesterday. Today.

Ink-Stained Love

Anne Dandurand

At first she wrote for desire, possessing him with pen and ink. And she would emerge from her writing, moist and panting.

Then she wrote to exorcise him, obliterate him, and soon her throat would burn like a queen's at her lover's torture.

And when she had done everything with him, when her pen had signed the innermost folds of his handsome body, she hesitated, suddenly alerted by the resounding void about her.

It was so simple. She arranged to meet him the following Monday, and over instant coffee, she confessed the love brewed under so many words.

He opened his arms to her with the noise of a dungeon.

As Moist as Montreal

Anne Dandurand

A week before she met him, one of the most beautiful fireworks displays was set off above the city. Invited to watch the sky at the home of two homosexual friends, she sipped her white wine and lightly talked culture seated between the two charming fellows; then, back at home, partly for want of anything else to do, she carefully shaved off her pubic hair, leaving only a small triangular tuft on the mons veneris.

She masturbated at some length, first with her hands, then with her vibrator-specially-developed-for-clitoral-stimulation. Then with deliberation, she sat down in front of a mirror, her thighs spread well apart, and with a polaroid camera and flash, photographed her vulva. The result was not at all bad, perfectly pornographic. Her face was not visible, only the the tattoo on her left forearm. She put the photo with others of the same type into a very secret album she wouldn't show anyone.

A week later the hairs are beginning to grow back in and she feels nothing but an imperious need to scratch. She meets him in a bar where a small celebration for the launching of a T.V. programme brings them together with a number of others. Astride a barstool, she moves to the beat of the music. She watches him; he avoids her. She knows he is with an actress who has a husky, sensuous voice. Under her full satin skirt she is wearing garters and pink silk stockings despite the heat, and several times she has nonchalantly raised the light material to show him her thighs. She is as moist as Montreal on this summer evening. She lowers her eyes and steals a glance at his crotch, at his sex, so closely molded by the tight trousers; she blushes, and growing hollow with desire, imagines him naked, and her tracing her name across his skin. There is hardly anything she enjoys more than this inflammatory lust.

Finally she gets up, and on the tips of her toes whispers into his ear: come on, I have to fuck you, I can't stand it any longer. She leaves the bar without checking whether he is following her, and turns into the first alley she sees.

It is late; a feeble bulb dangling from the end of a wire gives out its yellow light and dancing shadows. She leans against a broken-down door, between two big garbage cans. It smells of rotten fruit and cat piss. She only has time to pull off her pink panties before she sees his outline at the end of the alley.

Finally he is in front of her, opens his arms, says nothing. She kneels down, and undoes his belt buckle, and with her teeth opens his zipper. He's not wearing any underclothes and has an erection as if it were his last one ever. She rubs her cheeks, her hair against his generous tumescence, and with a throaty laugh swallows the palpitating stalk. But he leans over her, and gripping her under the arms raises her up against him, kisses the base of her neck, the corners of her mouth, her whole face while his hand searches under her skirt, going up the pink stocking to the garter, where the skin is so silken. He plunges two fingers into her pussy; she trickles and almost faints. There is nothing she likes more than this rough tenderness. Someone could disturb them though. They hurry. She bends her leg around his waist, he holds her buttocks and gently impales her. He pierces her, burnishes her passionately, and she, no longer able to bite her lips, finally lets rip the yeowl of sensuous delight.

Hardly any of this is true; I am only writing it to excite you, seduce you, so that you'll love me. And so I can love you.

Journey

Louise Coiteux

There will be a break. She will turn her head quickly. In a single glance she will see that the light from the lamp is hardly visible. She will say to a friend: I am really eager to tell you all this and she would reply: I'm waiting.

It can't be ignored. A woman bursts out laughing in a motel room. From that moment on it is no longer important. That morning she could have gone back to sleep but she prefers to hold her ear to the window and perhaps hear the sound of footsteps in the snow or the plate cracking.

Something creaks. It is in the air, and fragile. It was supposed to break.

The coffee is getting cold. She forgets, she forgets that she should have phoned. So she goes out. Goes silently by the spot where the fence prevents her getting through. Little by little she increases her speed. Her step quickens, she runs into town. In the narrow gravel streets, where the air and the pebbles crumble, the skyscrapers grow as she moves forward. Yesterday she apparently misplaced her bicycle. She's definitely going up. She's going up a slope. Up there a park. The journey ends and the road no longer exists. Her finger slides over the globe of the world. It slowly follows the curve of the stream. The stream flows into the river, the river into the sea and ... She has a short memory.

She only takes one métro ticket. Lets herself be rocked by the wheels rumbling on the rails and imagines at the same time the noise of the prison doors creaking. And the métro starts off again.

There is a dense crowd at the bus terminal. So she watches. She watches the others watching her. She knows what they are thinking. They're saying no style and she could reply that it's all just an illusion, nothing is for real but she is still too small to talk, so she thinks. Then she goes out and is going to wait for the bus outside. It's different in the winter. To kill the time, she slowly follows the corridors between the bricks of the station wall with her index finger. Passage 7 or 5, passage 2 or 6, she can never remember and they tell her she cries for nothing when she's only afraid of taking the wrong bus or the wrong number.

She sits down comfortably with her one-way ticket. Through the window she sees a man looking at himself in a shop window, a new suit perhaps, the young man, unseen, unknown, in a wedding suit and a rented car. She holds her ear to the window. Her lace dress rustles; her stitched slip smells of mint. She runs her hand through her hair, over her ears, along her neck and draws on the steamed-up window.

Maybe it's a bird. A butterfly is stuck to the frost. And the bus heads off again. It is warm and the drawing disappears.

She sleeps.

Later they will say : Did you dream all that?

A door opens. A girl is embroidering a design onto her skirt. First she carefully draws the outline. Threads the eye of the needle with the thin nylon thread. Her hands tremble. She drops the needle. She tries again, the knot is too small and the thread goes through too fast, straight through. Finally she loses interest in what she was sewing.

In the other room the lighting is hardly visible. A girl is reading the dictionary. Closes it at the letter c ... This girl smokes too much. Too fast.

Pass me a cigarette, you could say I lose my memory at certain pages of certain gospels.

The other girl is a musician. A sheaf of music lies on top of a stack of books. She would have written notes in it. Black and white circles. Still, she would know nothing about music except a piano hardly visible in a distant memory.

A door slams. Another opens. Large mirrors cover the walls of a dance studio. The dancer bends to pick up the paper handkerchief into which the female pianist cried for a long time. She reads aloud notes written on this paper.

Case caserne....

This collector is concerned about saving everything. So she slips the memo into her sleeve. That's when she thinks she has to go home. Later she will turn out the lights.

The bus has just arrived. The little girl opens her eyes. He gets up. Takes her ticket, punches it.

PERFORATED THE SHOOTING STAR

PERFORATED THE LITTLE GIRL IN THE NIGHT OF TIME

It is 9:22 in the morning. Somebody rings at the front door. I don't answer, or rather I don't answer anymore. I am sewing. The satin lining of my jacket is always hanging out. Has come undone in certain spots.

Subversion and Passion: Reflections, Wanderings

Danielle Drouin

In this text there is talk of wanderings and contradictions. The right to contradiction. The right to do what you have to do when you think it has to be done.

I would like us to have this right *but also the courage.* Acting on our urges and our impulses at the very moment we feel them. Contradicting ourselves again and again, increasingly real women, honest in our contradictions. Able to contradict ourselves, in order to be true at every moment. Increasingly fascinated, uncompromising, impassioned. Increasingly free.

I would like us to be heroines of the daily routine. Practising daily subversion. All the time everywhere. No longer letting others take advantage of us, imprison us in an image. Refusing this at each moment, with each breath. I would like everything to be meaningful, amaze us, make us linger on. Still ...

Still, already I feel I am going to tell lies. One thing is certain, I won't give my name. I've been given so many names that I can't quite manage to name myself. *And I never say here, even when death passes by.*

*

The situation

Wherever I am I am in the way. When I was working in an office, I was never there in mind, so that when I saw 35 I would write 63 and when I saw 63 I would write 27 and so on. It was catastrophic and the worst thing was that I often lost the key to the toilet.

I sometimes have the impression that people don't really know what to do with me. I am in the way. In class I forget to raise my hand before I speak. And I never sit in the same place. That throws off the little organisation of their space that people automatically set up. When I'm bored I look out the window. The view is magnificent, overlooking the city, night is falling. And sometimes I laugh, all alone or with others.

I have with me a book by Michel Foucault, a book by Nicole Brossard, a book by Pierre Bourdieu, a book by Virginia Woolf, a book by Georges Simenon, a book by France Théoret, a book by Erving Goffman, a book by Shunryu Suzuki, a book by Michel de Certeau, a book by Rejean Ducharme, a book by Marguerite Yourcenar, a book by Roland Barthes, and magazines, comics, photocopied articles, etc.etc. It's rather heavy.

I get impassioned, enflamed, I talk, I reflect, I make mistakes, I work, I listen. But somewhat excessively, I think. *My problem is excess.* I am interested in everything and everyone watches me being interested. Someone is watching me. What do I care? Someone thinks he would like to shake her, grasp her, break her, make her get out of what he doesn't have access to and what she's so involved in. That's what he says. What do I care?

Out of phase. Never really where I belong. Not at work, nor at school, not in the women's movement, nor outside it, not in the street nor at home, nor in the straight bars, or in the others. Always between two fires, between two waters. Between the fire and the fire and the water and the water. I end up sitting for hours *frozen alive* thinking.

But that's how I prefer it. The uncertainty burns me but I can't do without it. In fact I think I like burning alive for people, things, ideas. And what would I do with my niche if I had it? I prefer to search and search, to wander and wander, to weep and weep, to love and love and to lose and to die if I have to. Having said this ...

Having said this I wonder what exactly the implications are of what I just said. It all seems both terrible and impossible to me. Unbearable. *But maybe I need the unbearable?* Am I the only one like this? Do you understand me? Do you believe me?

Greed

It's odd. Even though I only leave Montreal 2 or 3 times a year, I always feel that I am a flagrant impostor when I'm in the country. In one sense, nature irritates me immensely. It can't be taken away. And, in another sense, I think I find it hard not to be able to take any of it. When I see a tree I like, it's not enough just to look at it, touch it, stroke it; I would have to be able to bite it, get into it. It's not enough just to look at a lake, to ripple my fingers in it, I would have to cover it completely with my body. I can't just look at flowers, I have to pick them, put some in my pockets, eat some. I don't know how to behave in a forest. That is called greed. It is very ugly.

And it is never calm. Always as though it were a question of life or death. Whatever I do. When I am on a mountain, there is the wind, the vastness and me. It is beautiful, and I gaze around and drink it in desperately. But I cannot prevent myself insisting on the fact that everything in this world is important, that the mountain exists only while I look at it. And that, in the vastness that opens before me, *it is not clear which of the two would eat the other.* That's what greed is. It is not pretty; it is, in fact, quite ugly.

And even more so because that is also what happens when I speak, or think. I put my whole life into it, so it gets heavy, very heavy. Urgency, a passionate voice, the choice of the words I like and the moving gestures. It is never something calm and may well end up being overwhelming. For the others. I leave classes, meetings, discussions both worn out and highly charged. So I go dancing until three in the morning or I write or I cry. Or I do nothing, nothing, nothing. I sit, my gaze lost, in front of the television, on or off, it makes no difference. *I come to myself with this fixed gaze.* Do you believe me?

Exaggeration

I may as well say it right away: *I am the sort of person who clings to the flowers in the carpet.* I have always loved rugs, floor tiles, linoleum. Since my earliest childhood I have practised the habit of remaining motionless for hours studying the floor, following the design of the rug, understanding the logic of how the tiles are assembled. I learn the stains, the dirt, the worn spots, the rips by heart. And I rest just as heavily on one idea.

> Reality does not exist. What exists is the idea we have of it. There are several levels of reality and the idea we have of it, what we retain of reality, that is our reality. Our actions are often more a result of the idea we have of ourselves, our situation, than of our objective reality. On the other hand things must be named in order to exist. And it is significant that certain things, certain concepts exist in one language but not in another. Moreover, reality may be expressed by a single word in one language while in another more words are required. In New Guinea there is apparently a language that has eleven genders and twenty two pronouns of the third person. That's amazing.

I tell it to anybody at any time. *Just to see.* I listen. I wait. I do a lot of things like that, just to see. Although sometimes I shatter my life just to see.

Lies

Perhaps I ought to clear up the question of lies. I lie easily, and from habit. So, when I say *do you think I'm pretty* I'm saying *do you love me*. And when I say *talk to me* I am saying *love me*. In fact, perhaps everything I say should be translated as *love me*. It's appalling.

And when I say *anxiety is a possibility I barely acknowledge* that is a complete falsehood. I walk alone late at night, my throat always a bit tight. I chew gum to give me courage, a tougher look. A man approaches me to ask the time. My heart beats wildly. It's a pain to have a man ask you for the time when you're alone in the street at night.

It's also a pain to tell so many lies. Because if now I tell you that sometimes I suffer terribly just to write two lines you won't believe me anymore. And when I tell you that my heart too bursts into a thousand sharp points that rip my throat, perhaps you won't believe me either.

Fascination

I have obsessions. Voices. My own voice. It amazes me, frightens me and I like it. When I talk into a microphone (and my hand trembles a little) it goes around the whole room. Low and tender. It catches me off guard from behind, strokes my back. It nails me to the spot. Gripped and fascinated as always.

I lose control of my voice. It wants to seduce before I even think that far. It gets so low, so gentle, so throaty before I even notice. It knows my emotions better than I do. It follows them step by step, follows them to the letter.

You often say you like my voice. You call me to hear my voice. And one day, someone tells me he noticed my voice, I had a beautiful voice. He says he told me. But it's not true. Another day someone else talks about her fascination with voice and fascinates me with her fascination. People who are fascinated fascinate me. Those who are fascinated by me force me to love them. Certain parts of the body fascinate me. Hands. When you talk I look at your hands. When you touch me I close my eyes.

Contradictions

Sometimes I like to be alone, a stranger in a place full of strangers. Always standing, leaning against a wall, a bar, a column. Not smoking. *Just being there in my right to be there.* Existing in my space, in my right to exist. I like feeling the diffuse mass of looks, murmurs, smoke, where I am and where I'm not. I also like the close attention, the sudden glance. Eyes meet and everything's clear. A streak of lightning, an electric shock. Desire sometimes so strong that there is no need even to talk, or to leave together. Everything's been done with a look.

Sometimes I choose violence. I dress in black and in leather and am amazed to recognize myself so completely in my fantasies. My movements coincide. My eyes are dark, my legs strong. I will certainly not be pushed around.

I am in black and in leather but I wander through debris and decadence like an angel. I plunge into the sordid. People are walking over beer bottles, everything is dirty even the lighting which is growing excessively dim. And I stay purer than pure even when I shout at the drunk yelling in the corner to can it, shove off.

With the help of alcohol some verge on hysterics. *Each person takes his secret frustrations out on another.* Admissions, insults, tears, hate and fear rise to the surface. Violence multiplies by square centimeter; we breathe it in through each pore and I don't escape it. My voice has become as dark as my eyes. My mouth is aggressive, my gestures feverish.

And still you would gently murmur into my ear that you love me, you would still place your warm hand on the back of my neck at the exact spot you know, still you would ask me on your knees to be nice to you; I won't move. I will stay icy. Nasty and cold, for this evening I am a black angel *and a black angel stays alone at night.*

Sometimes I choose ritual. And you look at me, at my whole body, the whole length of it. You intimidate me and I no longer know what to do. So I cover your eyes with my white hand. Like a ritual. You take my hand gently and lead it to your mouth. Your lips on the veins in my wrist. An infinite tenderness that crucifies me.

A perfect ritual within the perfection of some of our meetings. My hand fits itself to the curve of your cheek and your hair smells sugary. The pressure of your fingers on my shoulder. Violence and gentleness and again violence. We crush our bones against one another, we gnash our teeth together, we plunge into one another's eyes and are afraid. *And I no longer know what to do.*

A ritual when I open my eyes and see your thoughtful head, in the morning or somewhere else. You are watching me, serious. My heart tightens and I don't know why I feel like crying. You make me melt, you break me, you shatter me, you hold me, you kill me, you eat my heart. And I no longer know what to do. *And I love you so.*

The look

I always come back to where I started. I admit there is something immensely wrong with my life. It is because of the glass bell. Sometimes I feel it so distinctly I could lean my forehead against it to feel a little freshness.

Sometimes I hear, I hear, but I couldn't say who it is or whether it is the echo of my own words. Sometimes too a terribly heavy and burning lump lodges in my throat of its own accord. At the moment when I break cover, I lose the lump, I hang on and flay myself alive.

She never talked about it but sometimes she would lose her head. Can't find her money, her keys, her book, in a bus but doesn't know where she's going, did she lock the door properly, has she still got her keys, did she forget to go to her classes, to work. Once she even spent an hour searching for the umbrella that she had just put into her bag. Completely wiped out that time.

My head often jams at a precise moment. I stay locked on some memory. A little girl cries. To say she's in a rage would be an understatement. She screams in her head. She burns everywhere at the same time. She wastes away right there.

However, if I look behind – *the photos* – I see only my serious gaze. And this look never stops weighing down my life. Serious, ruthless woman, you'd think everything concerns me. It's dreadful.

And still scenes of horror pass by at the least moment of inattention. Shattered skulls, burst eyeballs, tortured bodies lie in wait for me to close my eyes. How could I have allowed such a sea of horror to flow in my depths?

It's crazy; it makes no sense. Bursting, tearing myself to pieces like this. The death urge with infinite precision, infinite precaution. I am slipping, destroying myself. Don't even need anyone else. It's painful and at the age of 24 my body already has a major fault and white hair.

Do you believe me?

Wandering

My name is Blanche Dénommée (Named / Unnamed), but that is not important. My gestures are beautiful but not noble. I am too emotional to be beautiful, I stumble too often to be attractive. I am always wavering between laughing and crying and I don't know how to smile my marvellous smile that I have been told completely lights up my face.

When I am given a name, I remove this name, and it is even worse when I introduce myself. I construct and destruct everything as I go along. I've heard about a woman sculptor who, come summer, would destroy all the work she had produced over the year. I am my own sculpture that I am destroying with small strokes. *Don't love me too much for I am constantly destroying myself.*

I am charged up to the point of jostling myself and I hardly notice it. My fingers are electrified and I no longer even recognize my own hand touching my hair. I learn to set my feet solidly on the ground and I get electric shock upon electric shock. I want to touch everything at once, my fingers so feverish they make me tremble to the inside of my ribs. These ribs which bear the imprint of your fingers forever.

I could say that there is a scream at the bottom of my throat and surely of yours too. Annoyed voices, dampened voices. May the scream penetrate to the back of the eyes. The voices move me but I look at the hands. I am constantly seduced and I often seduce too. It's quite absurd. I try to seduce people, children, the wind and even things. I kiss books, I caress tables, I run my finger over cups, I lean my forehead against windowpanes, I lick the sheets, and I let my hair brush other people's sweaters. I drown myself in eyes, I lose myself in my breathing, and I forget myself in the warm breath from your mouth on my temple.

Touch me or I'll die. Touch me, call me, talk to me, love me. I tell you I am an abyss and you tell me it's true. So it is true! You get into my head, my words, my life. And I hate you for it; I want to see you dead. It's diabolical but I can't help it.

I could tell you that we often walk down noisy streets. That it's windy and that there is dust in our eyes. There is also dust in our mouths we talk so much. We talk so much we don't talk to one another. I tell you the exact opposite of what I want to tell you and besides, you misunderstand everything. So we run our lives holding each other tight, hurting each other. We are totally, dramatically parallel. When we meet up, we collide. What do we want when we go to see each other? I really don't know.

And I often give in to the irresistible temptation of pushing everything to the limit. The arguments and the tension. It has to blow, explode, hurt. And it does hurt. Then I panic, put on my coat, leave. You sit there, staring ahead. Should you have been the one to get up; should I have been the one to stay there? In any case it is impossible to love me.

Still I always try to tell you things, my things. What does that mean to you? *We always have to pull the words out of your mouths.* There comes a point when I stop caring. I don't ask you anymore. Too bad. I don't like asking.

Instead, I take, I give. Whatever may happen, I don't ask. Pride and fragility? Or zen in the way I do what I have to when I have to? I say things as they are. I kiss whoever I want whenever I want if he, or she, also feels like it. I invite whoever I want into my room, into my embrace. *But nothing is sure.* I may do it tonight, but tomorrow nothing is sure. Will we see each other again? will we die together? will we love each other to death? or torment each other to death? We know nothing.

And perhaps you will tell me that these are all lies. That the truth is I am a beautiful woman dressed in black with mauve gloves. A woman one could love passionately. Sometimes that is true. And then I change my mind, I change my shoes. *I am no matter what, dressed in no matter what and I say no matter what.*

For days I go through rows of houses, rows of books, rows of beer bottles, rows of glances, rows of things which I don't remember at all. Rows in disorder and I feel considerably disrupted myself. I end up sitting for hours with fixed gaze. I get up, I go in circles, I sit down again. I change my field of vision, I lie down under the table, I roll down the stairs. I watch my plants dying of drought and I don't lift a finger to water them. I make tea and forget to drink it. I put on my coat but stay in. I am dying over you but I tell you I don't want to see you anymore. *I do whatever comes into my head and don't give a damn.*

In fact I'm skirting things. I make a thousand detours for fear of leaving too many traces. But hourly I come closer to myself and I tremble. The moment comes when I could grasp hold of myself, catch myself, corner myself. With slow, careful steps I get to myself and I quake. My own cold, white hands are already tightening on my throat. My fiery eyes hypnotise me at the curve in the mirror and make me tremble in fear. Already I feel a hot breath on the back of my neck; it is my own and makes my teeth chatter. I fix myself, motionless. I lean against the wall and wait for myself. I wait for myself and tremble. It will be terrible.

Walking

France Théoret

She is there perhaps when she displays vivid all her wealth outside. She is there like, always like, as, meaning, stopping at who is there and opens herself outside a reversed dream, she lends herself generous, she offers herself complete, she goes beyond, she emerges, she signifies without weighing heavy, she presents, she does not rarify herself by any substance, she sheds light, she leads on and gathers, she wanting it to be and it is, she includes, she comes to light, she by what she inflames without forcing, she made-up or not, she at the departure and the arrival of things, she is walking and can be seen. She is beautiful without symmetry. She nuances every spectrum, she leads to confusion, she lends herself in a few minutes and makes shame quiver as though this shame could feel shame. And it is not shame that is ashamed, those responsible are never besplattered. A life spent in avoiding splatterings. She is not hurt either. She is walking light and relieved of all weight. She knows without having learnt to walk. She goes about it with a long stride the length of long legs. Long arms too. She gaits and unrolls on the sidewalks the cadence of some woman who has learnt elsewhere and seems to know no one will ask where and she will not tell either. She is constantly prospecting the echo of things, most often an apple's or sometimes some fruit's, she asks for a hot milk. She is not hobbled by crevices, she is of tall stature sure of being a sylph and never sure of being assured, she does not at all want to be assured of anything, she is walking and about her things go on in the street full of four o'clock in the afternoon rue Saint Laurent. She is the very walk of a woman child tall and relieved of all thickness. She would repel rather than attract, she is pure vector, a living sign that lies exist. Lies and even murder are there, milling around and walking like she is. Everyday we kill someone, something of the other within ourselves. She is the detector of lies and crime. They burn to give themselves away as she passes by. She is wearing clothing soft at each step to fold beneath her arm, her leg. She has the honesty of the dead who fell silent and the beauty of Egyptian profiles. She keeps totality for totality. She cannot fragment her body and generates no desire in the voyeur, she embodies her clothing and it is so rich that her slenderness is incorporated and becomes the stuff of dress, or coat. She is naked even when dressed, only elsewhere is there surplus and entanglement. There is no ulterior motive either. She starts from a fruit, she moves a step, she grows with each movement, she does not separate herself, she does not judge, she sees into what cannot be seen, she is doubtless reflected in the pupils of the passersby who close up again immediately. She has no other reason for existing beyond her own existence. She is made of all the calm and all the silence of the best days. She is clothing and nudity, make-up and face and constantly movement. She is the going-toward whose destination we will not know, she walks in order to walk, she exists in order to exist, she forms under each pressure and would take root everywhere but doesn't anywhere. She is gently and feverishly mortal. Her delicacy has about it no delight that we could name, she offers herself in a thousand sparks without offering herself and never seeming to suffer from opening herself so far with no inside nor outside. The shape only and made even more for the ear. Tall, she is a miniaturist, she has the delicacy of a Japanese garden but she renders no service. Except to exist and act unknowingly like a developing fluid that reveals human violence. We don't know what fruits she may be eating or hot milk she may be drinking even though she does not want to sing the praises of the anorexic. She is dressed, she wears make-up and in this blend whose style or origin we can never really distinguish with certainty, she escapes from clothing and make-up. Similarly, she is clothing and make-up of an order without order which makes her completely irresistible and at the same time provokes every resistance. She sets up without setting up, incorporates without incorporating, she delivers up only her breath. Still, she is profoundly immodest and open. She is the impure itself for the ambient signs resonate on her. For the camera eye she makes cuts and has no effect other than her exclusive movement. She inverts the signs. She overturns impressions. Neither wild, nor tamed, full of holes right through the city. Fabric too. She is the live place, the knot and the clash. She shifts thoughts, like. From a line of dots. Details, burns and wounds. And yet her solidity is real. She makes what happens around her happen it only moves and passes on and stains like the dot of light vibration signal. She is the small animal of the dream, the prey we would expect to find easily cracked and crumbled. She opens the other dimensions: tall, she is lilliputian and moves about within the ear. Secret and there is nothing more offered and impure. She is the dream of heavy memories inlaid in the bodies of the passersby. All violence and all superstition speak their names before her. A prey she has no shadow. Global. She is the object of rites and never attends the rituals. She is the underside of the world born to the world who confuses by her existence for in her turn, she is big with births, with the unspeakable, the unseen. She believes she sees the crevices and breaks and would live with them if around her everyone respected their own wounds. At the high point, she lives herself profoundly on all surfaces. She favours modulation and outside. Colours conspire with the life of the folds. She makes do with any that form and leave room for matter and suppleness. Decoration is the substance and the infinite slippage of the great and the small which at every moment instills the desire to resist and the emotion which regenerates, induces seduction just to go on. She has suckers everywhere and everywhere she continues the unique walk of a living woman. She coincides with her line, the few rash and tenacious points that bind her ephemeral to the city. She, there, completely superficial. Porous and dangerously opaque too. Inessential in fact. Reflections. She arrives at the right moment. She offers herself gravely in the certainty of being mortal at each step. She bears the passersby in her ear.

Sunday

Carol Dunlop

It is only today and still ... you melt on the other side of this gaze, you raise your eyes and you know that never before have you dared to live to this point. A little later – much later in fact: you made love for centuries and hours, inebriating each other endlessly, gently, and with an accord always renewed in the original rapture, letting you drift with this immense swell; you caressed and loved each other in all ways possible; each one saying to themselves: this isn't possible, even going so far as to say it out loud, but within the intimacy; and the gaze captures you again and you embrace at length, gently and the gesture with which you touch his hair is not without sadness: you know very well that this kind of encounter occurs somewhere else, always farther away and suddenly you profoundly know one word, intensity, you are living it to its innermost recesses; too late, you have accepted its dangers for a long time now, you open your eyes and in all this time your fingers which had not stopped moving, have not yet reached the end of the gesture, the end of the brown lock of hair.

You sit up in the half-light, light a cigarette and listen to his breathing, you are happy: his sleep is gentle and calm. You get up and look at him, you bend over the bed for a long time, and you feel that never will a movement contain you more completely than this motion with which you curve and straighten up above the quiet form. You watch him sleep; never before have you known this desire to hold someone always in your arms; never before have you understood that you could do it with nothing more than your gaze in infinite solitude; no, you know that you have never before experienced such gentleness and it is growing, amplifying, filling you, overflowing; with endless sadness you turn on the light in the bathroom and take a long shower, while everything in the room stays quiet, but isn't there beyond all this the plane that you have to catch soon and that your thoughts are sending deliberately to the bottom of the sea, isn't there an endless list of responsibilities to fulfill for those of us who were already alive yesterday? And still his indelible presence deep down within you ...

Alarm, coffee; but no, it's evening already. Motionless and sad you struggle trying to keep a calm smile in front of this man whose finger brushes your cheek; impossible; the deep sob at the bottom of your throat and then its rupture under your skin; you have to look away and he isn't, never will be fooled; and even though you feel somehow that he is not the one threatened by such sadness you are not certain; and you know that once he has gone your anxiety will increase, your cry will find a voice or else have to be suffocated by some death or other, and there is a big black hole between your eyebrows; you press your head against his chest but the hole cannot be filled with his warmth and awkwardly you get dressed and follow him out, it takes you an eternity to put things in bags, proofs into an envelope, glasses into their case; and haven't you forgotten your toothbrush or something else and then, you look back to check everything over one last time and you see a huge damp stain spread over the wall, and it is as though a mushroom were taking root in your body, irrevocably, and in the corridor you again feel the ambiguous presence of ghosts behind the doors while doors and handles seem to be multiplying infinitely and again you wonder why you live here, in this neighbourhood and this house; the ghosts whisper in mocking tones and out in the street the danger presses closer without becoming clearer, you hold back a scream and he has felt all that and holds you by the hand, but you are angry with yourself because now his sadness spreads out above yours like an umbrella.

In the same métro carriage a woman turns slowly and stares fixedly into your eyes. Above a body that is still youthful is a death's head, a face white as wax and holes in the place of eyes, but these holes are eyeing you and expressing something that you perhaps refuse to understand, but you know full well that you have understood everything, that from now on it will be impossible for you not

SUNDAY

to understand; for the space of a moment you become a statue, not of wax but cold marble, and an immense fold crosses the macabre face as with the same slow movement the head turns and you know she is laughing an intolerable laugh, only you are deaf.

You follow him like a sleepwalker and on the platform you see the passengers enclosed once more in an envelope of yellow light pass by, continuing on their way, and no woman looks like the one that you just met; she is not on the train nor on the platform. You vaguely open your mouth as if to explain to him the reasons for your sudden pallor, but you stop: what could you really tell him? Again the sadness mounts and going up the escalator you tell yourself that you have never been as happy, and at the top of the steps you see a black grid and behind the grid a red stain, a stain like blood, and the last steps demand a terrible effort, inhuman strength would be necessary to get up them and you briefly look at this tall companion and you would like to warn him, prevent him from looking but the danger is gone, in his gaze you see (only) a red rag, or an old handkerchief or a piece of scarf ... As though such things were normal! And perhaps they are in this city where you regularly come across some kind of small rug rolled up and soaked with rain at the edge of the sidewalk.

You walk by shop windows inhabited by black mannequins dressed in white: congealed and stupid they hold their grotesque positions the whole length of the street, their bald shining heads get tangled in these steps you are forcing yourself to take on as your own; you know that if you stop moving you will immediately meld with these vague reflections of the recent rainfall lit up by the streetlights on the pavement.

Finally at his place and you feel that your absence, this inexplicable sadness and your hesitation before each breath bother him, and you feel you are not in the right place, you ought perhaps to float by the edge of his life, you don't know how to take off your coat, where to put your boots, or sit down; but the orderly peace of the apartment reassures you and you realize that this anxiety did not concern him, that no danger weighs on him this evening and you feel a little ridiculous, you sigh perhaps and you ask to listen to

Mozart piano sonatas, and somewhat cowardly, you open to the music, take a glass and relax for you know the moment is eternal; you look at him and the smile returns, as honest, as gentle and complete as at the beginning and you tip your head against the leather chairback and let the freshness penetrate you, and when you need to, your lashes sweep away with an imperceptible flutter, other scenes taking place at the same moment; you console yourself if necessary by telling yourself that this simultaneity itself, perhaps, justifies your incalculable resignation, and you will find out soon enough who this distress belongs to. Tomorrow, if it's by telegram, later in the week if it's by letter.

Excerpt from Picture Theory

Nicole Brossard

In the bar of the Hilton, the dancer from the Caribbean says, you will probably remember Curaçao because of a detail (Anna, who I had met by chance a few hours earlier had warned me that one reality does not necessarily fit over another but as flight attendant between Venezuela and Aruba left her to be desired). So it was with each phrase or in the casino (what followed made a woman say, it is late) when, with haggard eyes, I went from table to table. Only two women were staking bets.

From instinct and memory I try not to reconstruct anything. From memory, I initiate. And that cannot be from childhood. Only from ecstasy, from a fall, from words. Or differently from bodies. An emergency cell as it is body at its ultimate, unknowingly, the tongue will tell it.

When Florence Dérive entered the Hôtel de l'Institut, Montreal, 1980 rue St. Denis. Sentence fragments on the inside. At the reception. It was night. Since <u>Finnegan's Wake</u>. It was night. Florence Dérive, itinerant and so much from a woman. Brain ―――― memory. Night, numbers and letters.

Florence Dérive sometimes repeats a certain number of gestures that survive like writing and each time she displaces their ardour and meaning. Now Florence Dérive is going over her text in a bar at the corner of Seventh Avenue and Forty-Second Street. For the moment she is giving in to the need to be what is known as a character in writerly circles. Her lecture is ready. Tomorrow, Montreal.

Text / to cover, I feel its effects. In order to describe exactly a single reality born in complete fiction. *The white scene* of May 16. It was only in the waters of Curaçao that the idea struck me. With words, the same words, here, I will make progress since writing is the continuity of similar knowledge, an instinct for dignity amid what the styles think, beastly.

Florence Dérive, child of her mother and an ULTRA-MODERN New York style often spent her vacation at the seaside, at the house of her anarchist sister, the sole heir of the maternal grandmother. A house seen again and again from high angle shots by most of the surveillance helicopters which made the rounds of houses that might be sheltering bandaged men during the Vietnam war. The power to change America.

Florence Dérive, child of an ultra-communist Austrian mother wrote there are many women around us who share the same opinion. The sea does not have that many secrets. Then there was the shadow of a doubt so many words cast: what form do they take?

John, the son of the Austrian New Yorker had married the daughter of a protestant minister. Raised in Quebec, Judith Pamela grew up near the border. *male character, John had no notion of the novel.* Still with his dollars, a director and unionized woman proof-readers he built a lovely publishing house. For his wife – a novel.

Oriana, a long-time friend of the family, would often visit one or the other. She would tell Florence about the cinema, windows, cries, fascism, the stress on a conformist attitude.

Oriana, John's complicity, made sure he was a subversive son on the horizon of the New York streets. It was a difficult plan to carry out but Oriana chose to compete with the Austrian, Jewish, communist mother in the field of identities. And John would one day become what he was – a virile son.

Hotels grow old like models sure of their glorious architecture somewhere between the multinationals and the dirt accumulated on the Grecian columns in the LOUNGE. There's drink and discussion, though as tourists. Broadway / porn / Gestalt. Florence explained to Oriana, but a Corvette SOUND TRAFFIC, that love between anarchists and especially between women. A woman in the street turned around immediately.

Intention and fervour do not make a text nor a woman of me. It makes the individual body which at times borrows correspondence from desire move in double forms. Coincidence. Appearance. Each time Florence Dérive says in the bars as she does in the letters: 'womanal) /.

the / I familiar force is desire to me so similar. I say <u>after</u> <u>the</u> <u>text</u> and the statement rises from the body of a woman to a woman thinking. Dreaming is an accessory to writing. An anecdotal effect that swallows up great passions. That evening, it is in the Caribbean that I shiver the most. Without thinking I look at the sea, the Dutch dolls. In full sunlight.

Oh! the first chapter. Should I say: bandit skin and proudly stylish. The patriarchy will not take place, need I say it? At the VELVET SNACK BAR, Oriana, the complicity, says to Florence, as though it were still important: 'You know John worked a long time and cried a lot over his already discussed novel.'

The telephone. I get a line quite quickly.

Boulevard Saint-Germain, the Madison, waiter, elevator. Room: Flaubert exactly at the spot where it says that Paris is deserted because it is so hot – a vacation at the seaside, in the anarchist sister's house. Outside the bars are rejuvenated as quickly as the books in the bookstores. It was like humanity outside, they would often sit in the café humanity, that they observed with lots of descriptions in their eyes.

I got up very early thinking that it was best not to die doubled up like a hair on a pillow. A man's voice somewhere in the hotel was reciting a poem in a foreign language. My first impression was that he was having a discussion. I had breakfast. Then from one shopwindow to the next in the rue du Dragon, I got the impression. Echo: 'La Rivoluzione non è che un sentimento.'

Their Austrian and communist mother said that as a Jew she felt she was a woman and an intellectual. On the wall I saw the photograph of her when she was twenty. I saw a photograph of Florence and John with her grouped around a virile man. I saw memory in action. A photo of Florence and John at a demonstration. I saw the second cousin, poster-blue, Chicanos, grapes on the wall of the house at the seaside. The guest room. The

immense verandah overlooking the sea, where each time I watched lightly-dressed women on the pleasure boats.
Florence Dérive – New York-Montreal – that evening. Dawn, the ring of the alarm clock: day of the lecture. Subject: women and torture. Hôtel de l'Institut, sunny day, Carré St. Louis. SMOKE GETS IN YOUR EYES. The patriarchal machine to give you the blues. A little later in the day, Florence Dérive phoned Danièle Judith. That evening, she ends her lecture: in summary, it is easy to see that determined by writing, they were able to imagine that every woman must be put in service to a man, whatever her rank, whatever her sex. Silence: the audience grows excited.

Hôtel de l'Institut, Sandra Artskin, a protestant who writes marvellously without her mother ever bothering her simply in order not to confuse her with another woman *whose lightly dressed body*, passed by in front of the hotel. Text / I still feel its effects the day after when I am at the horizon from the window.

The white scene

to reconstitute would be the admission of something that could be only in fiction transformed by time. Still, there we were, the horizon, I will never be able to recount it. Here on the rug, intertwined, women. Visible. That is how I tried to understand the effect of the scene. And then without ever later having to nuance it. Imperative grammar burnt. I think about this scene like I do about the seaside, energy is no secret. She added: 'The moment is brutal and demented.' Contour, I speak its intensity, the living force like a cliché: the repercussion.

the other scene: I wait for her to return with the book. I wait for the book. The book is there, in my hands, the lips are ready to speak in an unexpected way.

a (1) Somewhere in the book the man's hand was placed on the woman's shoulder. They were walking like a couple, interminably on the stones, rue du Dragon.

a (2) The elevator was poorly lit. The man's jacket brushed against the stop button. He was watching the floors go past right in front of him (a blond woman was with him, watching him at shoulder level) depicted.

Full moon, Greenwich Village, John staggers. The city self-destructs in his eye. Life comes with the fog, trances, panic, rain, you forget everything and begin again: children, the minister, your novel. SEXUAL HARASSMENT. WHO DO YOU THINK YOU ARE? He followed the boy onto the quays of the Hudson River, where among men, torsos are con-fused. Elevator, waiter. Black out. New York.

Florence ends her lecture. Cigarettes, conversations in the foyer. At the restaurant a very beautiful woman says: the torture of women, I understand, yes but men / Florence Dérive lost in thought replies that in Los Angeles there are only men and therefore no torture of women. *Bens Delicatessen* never closes in people's minds.

Danièle Judith, traffic is heavy. We talk in / of profile like a statement of civilisation that marks a stop. '... we are short of manuscripts since the death of the ambiguous patriarchal hero.' *It was absolutely in another book* that she would be able to retrace the lines of a perfectly readable human figure when the moment came.

Florence Dérive, on Jane Street, back in New York, perhaps already writing, thinking like the thinking women that I saw and liked to observe maturing an idea in a salon while within them rose *particles of truth* that were hard to understand and they confronted in hand to hand linguistics. Here and there suffering, joy. Florence Dérive is like a woman who grasps the fact that it is absolutely necessary to resolve the question of intensities but especially the one which, splatterings, bloats women until they lose their breath and the sense of duration.

Paris. Métro. Métro entrance. Waiter, shackles, staircase. Livid. Freeing oneself from the code of aspects and asperities.

Since *Finnegan's Wake,* May 16, the white of the scene. Abstraction encourages the future as it does reality. Seeing: infraction / reflection or hologram. Each time I lack space on the horizon, my mouth opens partially, my tongue finds the opening.

The white scene

> I am adding on: so there are two scenes. One dated May 16,* the other shortly after. The book scene, the rug scene. Women fastened to one another as though held in suspension by writing, we exist in the laborious creation of the desire we have no idea of. Or in the creation of the Idea, anything that succeeds in transforming mental space. A sort of prerequisite the Idea to remind us that there are relays. The white scene is a relay which persists as writing while the body dictates its clichés, closes its eyes over the mouths that open repeatedly touched by fate in their own movement. Faced with what is offered: the extravagance of surfaces, transparency of the holographed scene.

Her mother's child, Florence Dérive was a studious girl: of mother born, she is reborn each time in the deadly streets of the city. AT FIRST A FIST. The father is a dangerous path. The city via history. Florence often talks about her mother facing humanity when humiliation cuts into her very belly. Heel. Florence Dérive sometimes takes on hysterical airs after reading certain books.

John drives smoothly along highway 95 in the direction of Maine. Wife** and children in tow. Chatting. Without this aspect of talk where would be the fantasy of the waves, the noise of colonial dining rooms, the shape of a shell? Expressionlessly John drives quickly his blood-red profile jagged like a landscape under the rising sun.

* This morning even the foyer is sunny. There is a persistent smell of wood. An aroma of coffee too.

** Judith Pamela liked travelling and languages. Flaubert was her favourite woman.

House viewed from the sea. View over the sea. Florence Dérive rests like a happiness index that gives access to pleasure: very far removed from the dictionary. Florence forgets her mother and the photograph I saw, the one of a virile father without too many muscles, freshly shaven. Another one of him, too, in the trenches. John has seen only men lightly dressed and helmeted. Caught in the trap of his vision. Seduced. Stuntman in the subway of dreams (his head in his hands): MY GOD! The photograph of a man in a photograph violently excites those who recognize themselves as deserters for he knows the deserter is alone and virile too.

b (1) The man's hand touched the woman's neck somewhere in the book. The man walked like a man, his interminable smile accompanies him.

New York: *Wine and Spirits*. Florence Dérive writes: the concrete hunger of the after-sun or the improbable pain, let Aruba arrive, let water, let matter come, at this moment I only know the body exposed to sleep.

Pages and lines of reflection: CURSE / CURVE gaze glass, every whirlwind that leads to the essential lip of my love: Curaçao, you reread your notes, it is late – I know – there are islands above Arizona arrives in distress in a text ——— skim over.

The runway on the screen, a strange linearity in the flight of fear. The newspaper you read before take-off: bomb, gold, mentality. There are areas that lie in wait for aerial memories. In the porthole the utensils make tautological reflections: cities still surprise me, repeated. Luminous. 'an image is a stop the mind makes between two uncertainties.' *

In the foyer of the hotel there is a receptionist, a commissionaire, the chambermaid, an American tourist and two brown suitcases marked with the name Tom Zodiac, Australia. It is seven o'clock in the morning, Hôtel Madison, the boulevard is deserted.

* Djuna Barnes, *Nightwood*

The hotel smells of verbena. It may be the fruit of my imagination but it smells good like in Curaçao, Anna smelt of fiction, on her back, I am getting ahead of myself.

8 rue Brantôme,* the sky is gray. I enter the museum. The feeling of being a clepsydra in the room's darkness. Leaflet: 'In HOLOGRAPHY, the main element is the method of lighting ...'. A man is drinking cognac surrounded by glass. He is smiling almost or naturally, future and public, that will be strategically disposed of in the cities. When the moment comes.

There is always a hotel in my life to make me understand the patriarchy. To understand the most banal foyer, the smallest maid's room, the rented room, it will thus be necessary to describe them all. The laudatory flow of four stars in the bosom of the night.

The emotional ground in the small hours. It is Friday, at this hour, Florence Dérive is watching over her text in gray New York, facing her bookshelves, the determined face of Florence Dérive in front of the already discussed works of some American authors. When she is finished, Florence reaches mechanically for the coffee pot.

The next day, the Quartier de l'Horloge: the holography museum. The rain especially for tourists. In the open air in natural surroundings, although the expression was formidable. Like a trick in fiction when the text sways, I walk in the direction of the foyer.

The white scene

the café first. Quotations since the booked rooms are filled to overflowing with books. Successive lapses of memory. Silence, a pensive reflex that returns bodies to their pleasure in boldness. This pleasure in oneself concerns terribly the work of formulation that one body undertakes with regard to another in order to come

---

* 4 rue Beaubourg, Sunny day. Deserted morning.

together by a movement of thought. The pleasure in boldness is unequivocal: it is transparent. What makes it difficult, is the total and irrevocable admission; this transparency that the body carries within itself like a personal history it relives in a decisive gesture. This gesture can be a movement of the hand toward a breast, the body or to directly touch the sex. There is always clothing that intervenes and that fits exactly with the extremely concentrated tension of the skins. Combined with the lighting, the pleasure in boldness dangerously dresses the body of the other in an existential layer that gives rise to the harmony condensed into an image which makes sense.

Oriana often returns from her travels at night. There is always a room waiting for her at the home of the ULTRA MODERN STYLE, communist mother. Oriana recognized by the doorman pushes the Penthouse button. An elevator like a computer. In America eros weighs heavy, torments itself, denies in other ways than by begging at subway entrances. It strikes like a livid orphan adopted by a housewife. It persists by a person's intervention 'something like that to keep the fiction going' (Roberta Victor) began as luxury call-girl at age 16 ...: 'The need for women to act out roles imposed upon them by society, to play the games and losing battles in order to still retain some authenticity are recurring themes – the actual themes of her history.' No 8.* The elevator opens at the apartment. It is raining. New York. A few grapes on a ceramic platter before going to sleep. Between two operas.

b (2) The man was looking straight in front of him at his fate on the door of the rising elevator. The metal faintly reflected his clothing without his face and the suitcase at his feet.

Basically, you say that each time you control yourself to prevent *the words escaping you.* Fiction thus thwarts unlilysybility / unreadability, in the sense that it always implies something more which forces you to imagine to double back. To come back.

* *Questions féministes*

NICOLE BROSSARD

A vacation at the seaside, on an island, where, when the sun sets, you would expect to see Ulysses break through at the horizon of the house (rose wood). 'The land of the Round-Eyes was there, quite near; we saw their smoke; we heard their voices and the sounds of their goats ... At sunset when dusk sets in, they stretch out on the seashore to sleep.' Deckchairs leave stripes on our backs and thighs. It is seven o'clock, Florence Dérive comes back from the village with mussels.

Café, francs. Cabaret, tight black pants. The waiter is obviously crazed by the night, standing in front of me. *The couch* is not far off. The city is a distraction from the writing causing me some thought. The city is this excess that takes hold of me like a vital exuberance and makes me juxtapose the sea and the buildings at the moment when alluding to early morning, in the rue de Buci, I try to write: I am making progress, making progress, she says to herself, toward repetition. I am making progress, she thinks feverishly in order not to stop at a shop window and see chained-up mannequins.

Boulevard Saint-Joseph, it is the doctor hour in the old private houses. Gynecologists, pediatricians, obstetricians. It is the hour for the profession of faith in Quebec. Danièle Judith is getting ready to read *Le Devoir*. In the street people are walking redundantly.

Ogunquit. Judith Pamela* looks in the book whose leaves she has not finished cutting, the sea. John's fictions spread out, kneeling in the sand building a lovely castle. Somewhere in Judith Pamela a memory works that does not hold her childhood and which still makes her stretch her whole body toward the water. The eldest fiction comes up to her, and places a butterfly on her cheek that is as imaginary as a kiss discoloured by the water at the uncertain horizon.

New York. In the Austrian woman's salon, into the midst of a conversation a young man quotes** a beautiful poem that no one among the guests wanted to expect.

* Judith Pamela is thirty and if John remembers (cf. fiction) has two children. It is hard and eternal like a poet who brandishes his verse.
** 'IT IS ALL NOTICED BEFORE IT IS TOO LATE.'

c (1) The man was holding the woman's hand in his arms. Like a couple, the man came back to each métro station, intact.

c (2) The métro was poorly lit. From behind, the man was hiding the woman whose hand was visible curled in his.

Nocturnal, Oriana sometimes allows insomnia to tempt her until dawn. Then she converses with John and Florence's mother. So beautiful, the Austrian woman, when she is brisk in the morning watering her plants. In her housecoat, very early, even before the sun rises, she may talk about her childhood, the war, her father. 'At first,' she says, 'when I was writing my first lectures, I would always set a photograph of my father on my work table.'

At the reception desk, credit card, signature. A green blotter. A taxi, the boulevard is deserted, a young man brings croissants in a wicker basket; he is sweating. The door: Charles de Gaulle airport. The city wobbles in the heat. The taxi driver looks straight ahead, rarely into the rear-view mirror; she seems to have a single eye trained on empty space, the very eye that makes the day coherent, three-dimensional and fictitious.

The white scene

the skins' transparency. In response to certain signs, in all fluidity, our bodies interlace compelled to melt in astonishment or fascination. Literally layers of each other at the heart of a radical motivation. The light of day. Such an abundance of light splinters the gaze. Eyes founder like a memory. Everything about this woman attracts me and words grow rare. Imperative grammar burnt, baroque eyes, I close them in profusion struck by the hypothesis that we have hardly moved on the rug.

At the seaside, time is sand. Judith Pamela thinks about the immense verandah that looks out over the horizon, where she could make silence and her thoughts come together, at this time when she and John are spending their holidays at the house of the anarchist sister* whom she hasn't seen for five years.

At the *Edelweiss* on Main Street in Ogunquit, John and Judith Pamela listen to the pianist improvise on the first notes of Lili Marlene. Around them men are chatting, brandishing their glasses when the refrain comes. Judith Pamela looks like a young mother: those among all the men who notice her look at her furtively, embarrassed as though they were seeing her again.

On the sand, dancers (of both sexes) mime the arrival of the pirates on the island. The Hilton is lit up. The glassed-in elevator goes up, two young people (of both sexes) on board. The pirate is dead. He is born again at the bar, circumstance or chance for a word. Anna passes by in front of me, arm in arm with a PhD. 'ALL SPACE IN A NUTSHELL.'

The show. The box where there are always flowers. Full house. Oriana: a golden helmet; you always imagine it to be heavy just like the shield. CURSE / CURVE / <u>all</u>**.

---

* The one who lives everywhere at once. Who often 'crossed' the border. A deserter too (most of them have become vegetarians and opened small businesses on rue Duluth, or in the mountains of British Columbia. In Nelson, their wives wear Marxist skirts and small hand-woven scarves. They all have two or three very lovely children who wander barefoot through 'natural food' restaurants).

** Stop father! Stop your curse!
Shall a woman bend and grow pale for a man?
Hoer unser Fleh'n! Schrecklicher Gott,
Spare her this bitter shame,
for our sister's shame on us then would fall!

Wotan

Did you not hear what I ordained?
I have banned your treacherous sister from your band;
No more shall she ride through the skies;
her virginal flower will fade,
a husband will gain her womanly favours,
henceforth she will obey her lord and master,
and seated by the fire will pass the distaff,

PICTURE THEORY

A rhythm is a rhythm. Florence Dérive sitting on the immense verandah before the sea, is listening to the tangoes of Carlos Gardel. The voice mixes with the sound of the waves. The daylight is blinding. Sweat all over the body. The cicada lets loose. Lupins, daisies, buttercups. Grasses.

Sandra Artskin actually went past the Hôtel de l'Institut that day. She was taking her manuscript with her, very proud that lightly dressed my mother didn't seem to care. Later in the day, she met a childhood friend. Sandra Artskin immediately recognized the other woman who was gravely listening to three men talking at a table. They looked at each other then embraced at length the lower parts of their bodies kept apart by the table.

When Florence Dérive left the Hôtel de l'Institut that morning, she noticed a young woman who, like her, had a school bag under her arm, doubtless bought at Bloomingdales, she thought at first, then she concentrated on a very specific idea she wanted to discuss with Danièle Judith before the lecture.

The poem screamed OF COURSE A ROSE IS ALWAYS FOLLOWING OPENING THE MIND. In the room at the Hôtel Madison I cry silently. Reality seen through the window is stunted. Taxi, a door opens. A woman in high heels gets out of the car and heads toward the foyer of the Madison. As always she could be mistaken for another woman. The poem was absolutely American, written at the Madison, my black coffee this morning (anarchy p. 185 – on a suburban wall) the curtain brushing the sentence, the clouds are deserted, I know you are sitting, bringing a cup of coffee to your

---

and the world will mock and deride her fate.
If her fate frightens you, then flee the condemned one!
Abandon her and keep far from her.
If one of you dare to stay near her,
To spurn my will and console her
that rash one will share her fate: she must know this!
Now be off from here. Keep away from the rock.
Hurtig jagt mir von hinnen,
or the same desperate fate will be yours!

All

Weh! Weh! Terrible, terrible! Horror! Horror!

lips, lightly touching the poem, this morning, when her voice called a taxi.

The style of each of Oriana's gestures on stage was expressive (enough). It was when she turned her entire body three times through the set that the audience got impatient. At rehearsals, Oriana would sometimes delay the sound while her mouth looked as though it was singing. Then Oriana would twirl until finally the song would continue. In the theatre, a white panic would grip the directors.

The poem screamed. At the end of the corridor a man is waiting for the elevator.

In the waters of Curaçao the whiteness is dazzling when you lift your head a little as though struck by the complexity of our thoughts, even the perspective that they can be complex. Then emotion tries to trick reality, melting it into oneself is a subsequent risk.

Full house. Oriana approaches the august father. Her breast rises. Her fate heard like a spell is vibrant. Aural flashes of lightning. Oriana sings, weeps, and submits. CURSE / CURTAIN / success.

4 rue Beaubourg. Sunny day. I enter the museum. A woman opens her legs while a girlchild floats in the space, still linked by the cord and the lighting.

Leaving the elevator I greeted the chamber maid who was looking at her reflection in the big mirror in the foyer. I left the key at the reception. I walked down the boulevard, then down another to the Seine. A woman sold me a postcard that I addressed to myself in Montreal, in the first café along my way, thus fixing this woman in my memory. The lovely expression of Greta Garbo.

d (1) The man was holding the woman close with his hands. The man's whole body trembled in order to keep the woman near him. Now a man's shoulder was hiding everything.

d (2) The man was holding the woman in his hands – a very small woman, drawn as with a knife on a terrace table as they watched her pass humanity in their dead eyes.

Passport, stamp, customs, Danièle Judith is waiting for me. To strive for the present, I listen to her closely. Highway, the Laurentians are inverted in my head as we drive to Montreal. In the rearview mirror there are few cars at this time of day. Fatigue stretches out: first chapter suspended between the mirror and the city.

The telephone rings (Florence Dérive arrived yesterday evening.) Despite my tiredness, I think of writing.) The apartment on rue Laurier looks like so many others. Work table. Sleep between the lines. Thus each sentence or what followed in the casino made a woman say: it's late, when with haggard eyes, I went from table to table.

<u>Feverishly I went for a walk in the streets of Montreal</u>. Back to the apartment. The answering machine: *This is Claire Dérive*. A lovely voice, almost no accent. In the waters of Curaçao, the whiteness is dazzling, and eyes half close to juggle the colours of the rainbow in the iris. I was obsessed by the voice of Claire Dérive, struck by an emotion and I voiced hypotheses in the bar at the Hilton, Anna a flight attendant, told me the story of her family or of her childhood spent in a shack in Puerto Rico near an American base. <u>She had said only her name</u>. Anna moves past in front of me. The pirate from the Hilton says: you will get a few details mixed up and it's only then that you will remember Curaçao and the Shell. Life instructions for use, with almost no accent.

We are sitting in the first row: it is easy to see that determined by writing, they were able to imagine that every woman must be put in the service of a man whatever her rank, whatever her sex. In the foyer we discuss. Then the scene in Bens Delicatessen. It is two in the morning. The sea has no secret. Oh the ambiguity, civilisation dreams or what in the idea succeeds in transforming mental space. Then the motor turns, I wait for her to come back with the promised book. The live force of the cliché: the embrace. Oh the first chapter, the tension the episode that fecundates. I try not to reconstitute anything, I initiate

Notes on the Contributors

HELENE LE BEAU is a Québecois feminist writer whose work has appeared in *La Vie en Rose* and *XYZ*.

MARIE-CLAIRE BLAIS is the author of *La Belle Bête* and many other novels. She has been awarded many national and international prizes, including the Governor General's Award for fiction in 1967 and 1979.

NICOLE BROSSARD co-founded *La Barre du Jour* and *La Nouvelle Barre du Jour*. She is a feminist theorist, and has published novels, theoretical texts, poetry and drama. She has won the Governor General's Award for poetry twice.

LOUISE COITEUX is a Québecois writer.

ANNE DANDURAND and CLAIRE DE are twins who are script writers, and publish regularly in literary magazines. They have collaborated in publishing a collection of short fiction, *La Louve-garou*, 1983. Anne Dandurand has also published *Voilà c'est moi, c'est rien: j'angoisse*, 1987, and her next book is in print.

DANIELLE DROUIN is a feminist writer from Quebec.

CAROL DUNLOP has translated works by Anne Hébert and Marie-Claire Blais. *Les Autonautes de la Cosmoroute*, written in collaboration with her husband, Julio Cortazar, was unfinished at the time of her death.

CONTRIBUTORS

SUZANNE JACOB is one of the co-founders of the publishing house Biocreux, and has published several collections of short stories and several novels.

MADELEINE OUELLETTE-MICHALSKA won the Molson Award from the Académie canadienne-française for her most recent novel, *La Maison Trestler*. She won the Governor General's Award for non-fiction in 1983.

LORI SAINT-MARTIN is a writer and works as an interpreter.

FRANCE THEORET co-founded *Spirale* and *Les Têtes de pioche*. *Les herbes rouges*, *NBJ*, *Liberté* and *Room of One's Own* are regular publishers of her work.

COLETTE TOUGAS co-published literary correspondence with Yolande Villemaire in *La Nouvelle Barre du Jour* and has published a novel, *Le Porphyre de la Rue Dézery*.

*

Luise von Flotow is a translator and feminist scholar. She recently completed a year of research in Germany, and is working on the translation of Quebec feminist novels and short fiction.

Beverley Daurio is a Toronto editor *(Poetry Canada Review; Love and Hunger: An Anthology of New Fiction)* and writer *(If Summer Had a Knife; Justice)*.

Other Fine Books from Aya Press:
1988 Gerry Shikatani
Hundred Proof Earth Milton Acorn
Love and Hunger: An Anthology of New Fiction
I Shout Love and Other Poems Milton Acorn
Utensile Paradise Richard Truhlar
White Light Brian Dedora
The Blue House Lesley McAllister
The Magician in Love Leon Rooke

For a complete catalogue,
please write to:

Aya Press
Box 1153, Station F
Toronto, Ontario
Canada M4Y 2T8